A sharp snick sent tingles down Carina's spine.

Ryder had racked a bullet into the chamber of his pistol. "I'm going to try to get us out of this with no gunfire, but it's best to be prepared."

Carina's stomach roiled. The sedan was inching alongside them, near enough now to make out the driver's face from the side-view mirror. Only, there was no face. The driver wore a grinning gorilla mask. Terror clawed its way up Carina's throat. She tromped on the gas, and the steering wheel went wobbly in her grip.

"Whoa!" Ryder grabbed the wheel, steadying the vehicle.

Carina heaved in a breath. "Sorry. The guy's wearing a mask. I've had a phobia about those since childhood."

Now was not the time to get into her kidnapping experience.

The other car crept up close again, and the driver's right hand raised up to reveal something bulky gripped in his fist.

A chill squeezed Carina's insides. "I think he's got a gun!"

Jill Elizabeth Nelson writes what she likes to read—faith-based tales of adventure seasoned with romance. Parts of the year find her and her husband on the international mission field. Other parts find them at home in rural Minnesota, surrounded by the woods and prairie and their four grown children and young grandchildren. More about Jill and her books can be found at jillelizabethnelson.com or Facebook.com/jillelizabethnelson.author.

Books by Jill Elizabeth Nelson

Love Inspired Suspense

Evidence of Murder
Witness to Murder
Calculated Revenge
Legacy of Lies
Betrayal on the Border
Frame-Up
Shake Down
Rocky Mountain Sabotage
Duty to Defend
Lone Survivor
The Baby's Defender
Hunted for Christmas
In Need of Protection
Unsolved Abduction

Visit the Author Profile page at LoveInspired.com.

UNSOLVED ABDUCTION

JILL ELIZABETH NELSON

LOVE INSPIRED SUSPENSE
INSPIRATIONAL ROMANCE

LOVE INSPIRED® SUSPENSE
INSPIRATIONAL ROMANCE

Recycling programs
for this product may
not exist in your area.

ISBN-13: 978-1-335-72308-6

Unsolved Abduction

Love Inspired
22 Adelaide St. West, 41st Floor
Toronto, Ontario M5H 4E3, Canada
www.LoveInspired.com

Printed in U.S.A.

He loveth righteousness and judgment:
the earth is full of the goodness of the Lord.
—*Psalm* 33:5

To the suffering victims of crimes everywhere—
especially the innocent children. May you be assured
that God's justice will in the end eternally prevail.

ONE

In the darkness of her bedroom, Carina Collins jerked awake, cold sweat coating her body. A scream welled in her throat but remained trapped within her clenched airway. The familiar nightmare always ended in that noiseless scream, just as the memories of her abduction when she was seven years old remained trapped in a deep, dark compartment of her mind. The psychologists said she might never recall what happened. As frustrating as it was to live with a blank spot in her brain, she'd learned to cope. With practiced deliberation, she relaxed her muscles one by one as she mentally recited Psalm 23. At last, the pent-up oxygen left Carina's lungs in an anticlimactic huff.

She lifted her head from her pillow and glanced at her clock on the nightstand. The illuminated numbers said *12:05*. Her gaze traveled around the unfamiliar room. Moonbeams stole past the edges of the window blinds and wrapped the space in twilight, barely exposing geometric shapes of unopened boxes squatting against the far wall. Where was she? Oh, that's right. The move. She and her toddler son, Jace, had relocated from Tulsa to small-town Argyle, Oklahoma, only yesterday for her new job as accountant at the local farmers' cooperative.

What had awakened her? Not the dream. A noise. Had Jace cried out?

Carina held her breath and listened. Silence from the direction of Jace's room. No, the sound seemed to float upward from the downstairs floorboards of the small, 1950s-era home she'd leased. All the walking through the house and up and down stairs yesterday, transporting boxes and household goods, had familiarized her with the unique moans and groans of the place. Surely she was imagining the stealthy tread. But the faint sound was too regular to be the random noises of a house settling. Then, that first step at the bottom of the stairs let out its arthritic complaint.

Her pulse stuttered. It hadn't been her nightmare-stirred imagination. Someone was in the house and coming toward her.

Chills cascaded through Carina's body, threatening to paralyze her. She sucked in a breath and shook herself. She was twenty-seven now, not a child, and she had a baby to defend. Carina flung off her covers and sat up. Where was her cell phone? She needed to call for help. Her gut clenched. She'd left the cell downstairs on the charger. Why, oh why, hadn't she brought it up with her when she went to bed? Too late now.

God, please guide me to protect myself and Jace.

Thankful for the worn carpet that muffled her footsteps, she hurried to the closet and flung open the door in silent haste. Reaching toward the overhead shelf, she felt for and found the case that held the Glock 19 handgun her late husband had given her three years ago—shortly after their wedding—and insisted she learn how to use. *Thank you, Dillon. I miss you!*

The old wall-mounted air conditioner that serviced the upstairs kicked in with a hum and a muted rattle. She had hoped for central air in a rental house and hadn't found it, but now she could be grateful. The sound would help cover any unavoidable noises she made loading the gun.

Heart pounding, fingers shaking, she fumbled the case open, located the full magazine, and inserted it into the gun. She did it all in the dark. Flipping the electrical switch was not an option if she wanted to maintain the illusion that she was none the wiser about the break-in. She'd wait until the intruder showed himself and then surprise *him* with her weapon. If the housebreaker was also armed, she needed the element of surprise to retain an advantage.

Was that a muted footfall outside her bedroom doorway? With the A/C humming, she couldn't be sure.

Too bad she didn't have the extra moments that would be available if the intruder needed to open her door, but since Jace had been born she'd never slept with her door closed—the better to hear him if he woke and fussed. Yes. A definite tread of someone stepping into her room. But she couldn't yet spot the intruder around the corner of the closet. The person's presence was hidden…silent…but terrifyingly real. And close.

Carina held her breath and gripped the coolness of her gun in both hands. Whoever was there seemed to have stopped just over the threshold. Who could it possibly be?

An image popped up in her mind's eye of her scruffy-looking neighbor. When she'd arrived yesterday afternoon with the moving truck following her compact SUV, the guy had been wielding a hedge trimmer on seriously overgrown shrubbery between their two houses. At the time, she'd thought Mr. Scruffy's hair needed a trim more badly than the bushes. A good barber and a shave might have rendered the thirty-something guy attractive. His deep blue eyes certainly possessed a riveting quality. Not that a pair of nice eyes and the breadth of sturdy-looking shoulders meant anything to her. She'd studiously ignored his unsmiling appraisal as she went into the house with Jace and remained there, directing the movers as they brought things inside.

Was her neighbor the person standing mere feet away from her now? Or maybe it was someone else entirely. Possibly even a woman. But why come up here? Why not just grab valuables downstairs and scram? Her gaze darted to her bed, shrouded in deep shadows, which was where the housebreaker's attention must be focused. Her wrinkled covers made a lump across the mattress.

Suddenly, the intruder rushed toward the bed, arms raised chest-height, hands clasped together around a bulky object. A distinct coughing spit sounded, followed by another. Carina's jaw dropped. What sort of strange behavior was this? And what had that muted noise been? She'd heard spitting sounds like that on television when an actor fired a silenced pistol. Had the burglar tried to murder her? The person leaned over the bed and let out a soft curse. Definitely a male, judging by the timbre of his voice. He began to turn toward her.

"Stop right there," she said. "I'm pointing a gun at you." If only her voice hadn't emerged like a squeaky teenager's through her taut throat.

The intruder dropped low with a rough chuckle. Laughing? How weird was that?

Carina threw herself sideways. That odd cough sounded again even as she pulled the trigger on her handgun. The explosion from the Glock erupted, loud and intimidating, but wherever her bullet had gone, it hadn't hit the intruder. He never flinched. Her shoulder met the floor hard, jarring the gun loose from her grip. The guy, rising from his crouch, was still chuckling.

Tingles scurried up her spine. She was done for as soon as her attacker pulled the trigger again on that silenced gun.

Jace, Mommy's so sorry to leave you. I didn't want to.

"Drop that shooter and get your hands up, or I'll blow you out of your shoes," a deep, authoritative voice commanded from the doorway.

The overhead light popped on and Carina

blinked against the sudden illumination. Her gaze riveted on the person who had tried to shoot her. The attacker was a nondescript, balding man, fortyish, of average height and build. His bland appearance, accented by dark-rimmed glasses, gave more the impression of a mild-mannered businessman than a killer. He was dressed neatly in black slacks, a black polo shirt and a pair of close-fitting black gloves. The would-be killer stared openmouthed at the newcomer to the scene. Carina swiveled her focus to him.

Mr. Scruffy stood a few feet from her, tall and sturdy as a tree trunk, aiming a shotgun at her assailant. Large, bare feet poked out from beneath the bottoms of well-worn, paint-spattered jeans, and his wrinkled shirt featured several buttons mismatched with the holes. A wild mane of sable hair tumbled to his shoulders. His clean-cut features hinted at handsome, but the generous five-o'clock shadow blurred a strong jaw. Yet those storm-blue eyes commanded attention. Bloodshot, yes, but not bleary—they stared down the attempted murderer with the kind of cold purpose only a fool would ignore.

Evidently, Carina's attacker was not a fool. His silenced pistol thumped to the floor and he raised his hands above his head.

"Kick it away," her disheveled rescuer ordered.

The man's lips compressed into a thin line, but he obeyed, sending his firearm skimming across the carpet, nearly colliding with Carina's dropped Glock. She inhaled a long, shaky breath even as Jace's wails began to protest the wee-hour commotion.

Ryder Jameson flicked a glance toward the petite, dark-haired woman picking herself up from the floor. No blood evident on her skin or her blue-flowered pajamas, so maybe she hadn't been hit, but he couldn't simply assume.

"Are you all right, ma'am?"

"F-fine… I think."

"Do you know this guy?"

"I've never seen him before." Her head swiveled in the direction of her child's crying. "Jace! I have to go to him."

The woman's wide, golden-brown gaze returned to Ryder and wordlessly pleaded with him, as if requesting permission. Of course, he was the only one in the room holding a gun at the moment, and in this disorienting situation—with him being a stranger—she couldn't be certain he was safe to trust.

"Go ahead." He jerked a nod. "I've got this until the police arrive. I called them as soon as I spotted this lowlife breaking into your house."

The woman's eyes widened and her mouth opened as if to ask a question, but her child's cries ramped up a notch. She clamped her jaw shut, brushed past him and scurried from the room.

Ryder narrowed his eyes on the gunman. "You're no burglar intent on stealing property, yet it took you next to no time to access the house through the rear deck door. Between that skill set and the silenced Ruger—" he nodded toward the gun "— I'm thinking you're a professional. Someone have a problem with the lady of the house?"

The assailant's mouth twisted into a sneer. "You handle yourself like a cop and talk like a cop, but you're not a cop, because you said you *called* the cops. I don't have to answer you anything."

Ryder snorted, ignoring the pang the gunman's words sparked in his chest. "Like you're going to speak up when *they* arrive either."

"Whatever." The man's nostrils flared, his slate-gray glare spitting flames, but he went silent.

Up the hallway, the baby's cries had subsided and the woman's comforting murmurs carried to Ryder's ears. Gutsy lady. She'd fought back against a murderous attacker, and the terror of the past minutes could hardly have started to fade, yet she sounded calm as a spring breeze with her child. Guess that kind of selflessness went with the parenting territory.

The wail of a siren drew close to the house.

Ryder sent a wolfish grin at his captive. "Let the party begin."

The man's pale face reddened.

Pounding sounded on the front door, as well as the familiar yelled identification as police.

"I'm sorry, ma'am!" Ryder called to the woman, "but you're going to have to go open the door before they break it down."

"I'm on it," she answered.

From the corner of his eye, Ryder caught her slim figure whisking past toward the stairs. The curly-headed toddler in her arms was again wailing, eyes wide and brimming with tears.

Poor kid. Not only was he trying to get used to sleeping in an unfamiliar house, but he'd been shocked awake in the night by a gunshot and now he had to cope with loud sirens, strangers in the house and fists pounding on the door. A muscle in Ryder's clenched jaw twitched. Still better than waking up with his mommy gone.

Minutes later, the would-be killer had been patted down, cuffed and led away by a pair of uniformed officers. Then another pair arrived in a second squad car. One of them confiscated Ryder's shotgun and shooed him out of the bedroom. The other started taping off the room, awaiting the arrival of the crime scene investigators who had to drive in from Lawton, over an hour away. Argyle's population of less than ten thousand was too small to maintain its own team of CSIs. Argyle's lead detective had also been roused out of bed to handle the case.

Gut hollow, Ryder trod down the stairs. He hadn't known being shut out of the law enforcement loop would drive his spirits lower than they'd already been for the past six months. How could they sink any further? Must be the aftermath of adrenaline rush.

Since he'd been asked not to leave the premises until someone took his statement, he went in search of his new neighbor and her son. He found them seated on a small sofa in the living room. The square space was dimly illuminated by a single lamp on a side table. From the doorway, a quick, instinctive scan found touches of order emerging from the chaos of moving boxes and containers that littered the room.

The little boy—Jace, she'd called him?—had settled against his mother's shoulder, sucking his thumb, eyelids drooping. As Ryder walked in, the child lifted his head, gave the newcomer a brief, steady look then settled his head on Mom again. At the kid's silent acceptance, a molecule of warmth blossomed in Ryder's heart.

The woman offered Ryder a tiny smile as he took a seat in an armchair opposite them. "Thank you is hardly adequate," she murmured.

"Glad to do it." He, too, kept his tone little above a whisper. The kid's eyes were fully shut now, his body as limp as a sack. Far be it for him to disturb the little guy any further.

"I'm Carina Collins, and this is my son, Jace." The child slept on through his mother's soft chatter as she rubbed gentle circles on his back with her palm.

No wedding ring on her finger. Not that the lack thereof was personally relevant, but the trained habit of picking up on details stuck with a person.

He leaned toward her, elbows on his knees. "I caught the Jace part earlier. How old?"

"Eighteen months." She smiled down at the little head on her shoulder.

"I'm Ryder Jameson. Sorry we had to meet under such circumstances."

"I can't argue with that." Carina grimaced. "But I'm glad you were around. How did you spot the break-in so quickly?"

"I guess there can be an upside to chronic insomnia." Ryder offered her a half smile. "I was puttering with a renovation project in an upstairs bedroom when I saw suspicious movement on your back deck—somebody leaning over the locking mechanism on your patio doors. It crossed my mind that it might be your significant other, Jace's dad or whoever, but then I realized anyone legitimate would come in the front door and not need to pick a lock."

Carina shook her head, the corners of her lips drooping. "My husband passed away of a sudden heart attack soon after Jace was born."

"I'm sorry to hear that." Ryder's chest tightened.

"Me, too." She offered him the steady, sad look of someone still coming to terms with grief.

Too bad he couldn't say the same thing about coming to terms with his own losses. Not yet anyway.

Ryder shoved the thought away and offered her a nod. "You said you weren't acquainted with the shooter. Do you know of anyone who might have sent him here? Someone who would want you dead?"

Cheeks paling, she shook her head. "I wish I did. Then the police could go arrest the person."

Her body language and facial expressions showed sincerity, but that answer didn't give law enforcement much of a foothold for investigation. Unless the would-be killer in custody was willing to talk. But he doubted they'd get much out of him. Ryder had seen lots of hard cases, and this guy struck him as stone cold.

He offered his neighbor a smile. "I'm sorry I wasn't able to get over here in time to stop the creep from gaining access to the house. It took a couple of minutes for me to call the police, grab and load my shotgun, and trot across the lawn. As it was, I cut it rather close, though you were doing the right things to defend yourself."

"I was about to fail." Carina bit her lower lip and looked away from him.

Her profile was striking—smooth brow, high cheekbones, slender nose, wide but graceful sweep of a mouth, dainty but firm jaw and a shell-like ear peeping through strands of wavy, shoulder-length hair. Yet it was the amber eyes, framed by elegant brows and long, thick lashes, that made her beyond pretty in a unique rather than a classic sense.

The woman met his steady look. "Thank you again, Mr. Jameson."

"Call me Ryder."

"All right, Ryder then. And you can call me Carina. I can only believe God had you in the right place at the right time."

Ryder's gaze dropped and he studied his bare toes. Why hadn't the timing worked out that way six months ago? Where was God then?

"You must be exhausted," Carina said. "And you've already done so much. Don't worry about us. We'll be fine. When the cops are done with our statements, you go on home. We've disrupted your life enough as it is."

Ryder's heart squeezed in on itself. He had no desire to depart. Why was he reluctant to leave these two? The bad guy had been stopped and caught. Yet, if he was correct in his assessment that the gunman was a professional, that left a person out there, unidentified and on the loose, who apparently wanted Carina dead. Would the individual try again, and if so, how and how soon?

Foot treads sounded on the old floorboards and one of the uniforms entered the room. The young female officer sent them a tight smile.

"Detective Worthing called and said I'm to take your statements and bring them to him down at the station. He's going straight there to interview the suspect. You'll probably be asked to come in to answer follow-up questions tomorrow. My partner is going to remain here for the CSIs." Her gaze zeroed in on Carina. "Is there some place you can stay until we're done processing the scene?"

Carina's eyes widened. "I have to leave my house? Can't Jace and I just sit here until the investigators are done?"

"Protocol, ma'am."

"Believe me," Ryder said, "the CSI activity is going to put Jace wide awake and keep him awake. They'll be traipsing through the whole house gathering evidence from the point of entry all the way up to the scene of the assault."

Carina inclined her head toward him. "Either you're obsessed with watching true crime shows or you have some kind of firsthand knowledge."

"He was a homicide detective and SWAT team member, ma'am," said the uniform. "A decade with the Oklahoma City Police Department. Outstanding record—decorations, commendations…ah, that sort of thing." The woman seemed to think better of finishing her sentence the way she might have intended to.

Ryder stared at the officer and lifted a brow. The woman offered a nod, gaze somber. He looked away from the too familiar sympathy. Of course, the local PD had done its homework on him, probably as soon as he'd hit town a couple of months ago. No such thing as anonymity in a burg this size.

Carina blinked at Ryder as if seeing him for the first time. His face heated. He steeled himself to field the questions that were sure to follow. Like why he was now holed up in little Argyle, apparently no longer on the police force.

She opened her mouth as if to speak but the radio on the uniformed officer's belt burped static. The officer swiped it into her hand and left the room. Jace mewled and stirred but didn't open his eyes. Carina subsided into silence, rubbing the toddler's back.

Ryder inhaled a deep breath at the reprieve from further conversation, but then he stiffened as the tone of the officer's voice on the radio turned sharp and urgent. He couldn't make out the words, but something was clearly wrong.

Moments later, the officer returned to the

living room, the tension in her jaw and around her eyes apparent even in the muted lighting.

Ryder rose to his feet. "What is it?"

"The detective said I'm to tell you…" The woman's eyes darted from him to Carina and back again. "The suspect overpowered the officers who were taking him to the station and has escaped."

The uniform's bleak expression and thready tone told Ryder there were awful details to the suspect's escape that weren't being told, but now was not the time to probe for specifics.

Carina stood and stepped up beside Ryder. "The man who tried to shoot me is loose?"

The officer nodded. "But we don't think he'd be foolish enough to come back here and try again."

"What if you're wrong?" Carina's voice was a hoarse rasp, as if she could scarcely get the air out.

She swayed on her feet. Instinctively, Ryder wrapped his arms around her and the baby and pulled them to his side. Carina's body trembled against his. He didn't blame her. Jace's innocent, trusting breath warmed his neck.

"I have a spare bedroom at my house where you both can be undisturbed and safe," he told her.

Steel wrapped around Ryder's spine. He'd

barely met his new neighbor and her son. No one would think it odd if he walked away from the situation—leaving it to the authorities who had caught the case—but his conscience wouldn't cut him that break. He hadn't been able to save his team the day his life was shattered. Now, nothing on this earth was going to stop him from keeping Carina and Jace in the land of the living.

TWO

Ryder's arm around her shoulder sent a wave of warmth through Carina, a temptation to yield that she would have to resist. The gesture was surely meant to comfort, but leaning on someone else was exactly what she couldn't allow herself to do when she was finally learning to stand on her own.

When Carina married Dillon, she'd practically had to fight her aunt Althea to free herself from the smothering nest the well-meaning woman had created for her when she'd taken Carina in following the murders of her parents and her abduction as a child. Then, when Dillon passed away, it had been too easy to fall back into the nest, returning to her aunt's house while grief had its way with her. Big mistake. Things had gotten ugly relationship-wise when she'd decided to take the job here in Argyle and leave Tulsa altogether, a move her aunt had fought tooth and nail against. Carina had remained firm and wasn't about to allow herself and her son to be dependent on anyone again.

She disengaged herself from her neighbor's gentle grip and stood tall. "We can go to a motel for the rest of the night."

The officer frowned. "You could, but the best we'd be able to do for your protection is to have a unit drive by periodically. Circumstances…uh, have got us stretched pretty thin."

Some sort of significant look passed between Ryder and the officer.

Carina caught her breath. "What happened to the officers who were taking my attacker to jail?"

"They're in the hospital, ma'am."

Carina's stomach curdled. "I'm so sorry."

"You've got a baby to think about, ma'am."

"Yes, of course. I see it would be better for everyone if I accepted Mr. Jameson's kind offer."

Next to her, Ryder stiffened, clearly noting her reversion to his formal name. She didn't mean to offend him, but she had to keep the guy at arm's length. How well did she know him, anyway? Then again, he'd demonstrated bravery and kindness, qualities that were far more important than externals like a shave and a haircut. Besides, he had police training.

It would be like protective custody. Temporarily, of course.

Surely this mess would be resolved quickly. Her assailant would be recaptured. And the authorities would soon figure out whatever—whoever—was behind the attack. Right? She desperately wanted—no, *needed*—to start afresh on her own terms. God wouldn't allow more tragedy in her life, would He? She'd had heaping helpings, and she only wanted to build a future for herself and Jace in peace.

"Is there anything you need to gather before we go?"

Ryder's gruff-voiced question jerked Carina from her thoughts. She looked up at him, offering a small smile.

Then she turned her gaze toward the officer. "I know I can't go into *my* room, but am I allowed into my son's room to gather his diaper bag, a few of his clothes and his favorite teddy? Nothing criminal happened in there. And I should grab his whole milk, juice and favorite cereal from the kitchen."

"Yes to entering Jace's room," Ryder said. "We've all been traipsing up and down the stairs anyway, but no to kitchen access. The suspect came in through there, and since he's escaped, any forensic evidence he left behind is more critical than ever. I think I've got enough things at my house that Jace can eat and drink. Oops! Sorry." He grimaced at the openmouthed officer. "Force of habit with the instructions."

The woman flickered a smile. "No problem. That's what I was going to say anyway. Let's get those initial statements now."

Twenty minutes later, the statements had been given and, thankfully, Jace had continued to sleep through the quiet conversation. Well, at least until the conversation turned tense when the officer seemed skeptical that Carina knew of no reason why someone would want her dead. Then Jace fussed, lifted his head and practically glared at them all. Properly chastised by an infant, everyone went back to murmuring. The moment might have been slightly amusing if her self-appointed protector hadn't also been eyeing her speculatively on the subject. How many ways could she insist on the truth? She had no idea why she had been marked for death.

Tamping down irritation that masked equal parts fear and dread, she collected items for Jace and a toothbrush for herself. With the movement, her son squirmed and whined in her arms but didn't open his eyes. At last, Carina followed Ryder out her front door into sultry darkness. It was after 2:00 a.m., but at high summer in Oklahoma, the heat of the day hardly faded at night. Warmth radiated from the sidewalk beneath her bare feet and the sweet scent of honeysuckle flavored the air.

The CSIs would arrive at any moment and Carina wanted to get herself and Jace settled into the promised bedroom at Ryder's place before any further activity in her house. Jace's little body had grown awfully heavy and he was letting out soft fussy noises. Hopefully, he would settle again if she laid down with him and cuddled him. They'd done that a lot after his daddy's death, finding comfort in one another. Carina had only just been getting him to sleep on his own in his crib again right before the move. And now—she heaved an inner sigh as she followed Ryder onto his Tudor-style porch—it looked like a backward step in that process.

At least Jace still *had* a mama. She needed to be thankful for that.

Wordlessly, her host led her up a hallway past a living room on one side and a dining room on the other. Light from a room at the end of the hall guided their steps. Ryder stopped short of the lit room and opened a door on the left. He motioned her inside a spacious bedroom that smelled faintly of lavender.

"Used to be my mom's room," he whispered

to her. "Help yourself to anything you need in here. The closet might even hold a few clothes that fit you, though I don't guarantee current fashion." He grinned, his teeth showing white against his dark scruff.

Really, she had to admit he was quite handsome beneath the dishevelment. And no, she shouldn't be noticing.

"Thank you," she whispered back. "We'll be fine."

With a nod, he closed the door gently. The pad of his bare feet retreated to somewhere else in the house.

Exhaustion hung like a sodden blanket over Carina's mind and body. Without turning back the quilted coverlet on the bed, she lay down with her son. The mattress was soft, but not too soft. A knitted afghan was folded across the foot of the bed. She pulled it over them both and closed her eyes. Jace burrowed close with a soft sigh and went still, eager for undisturbed rest.

You and me both, kiddo.

Familiar giggles drew Carina awake. Jace? She lifted her head from the pillow and glanced around. Her son wasn't with her. A couple of months ago, he'd learned how to wiggle himself, feet-first, safely down from an adult bed, though he hadn't yet mastered pulling himself up onto one. And now he was somewhere in the house, laughing.

What time was it? No clock was visible, but judging by the golden light peeping into the room from around the window blinds, morning had fully come.

Carina sat up as a muffled male voice was answered by another spate of toddler giggles. Her heart melted. Jace's laughter never failed to turn her insides to warm putty.

At least someone was in a good mood. As for herself, her mouth was a desert, her eyes were heavy with grit, and last night's terror seemed to have coiled somewhere in the pit of her belly like a viper waiting to strike again. It was like waking up from the familiar nightmare with no assurance that the events were in the distant past, over and done with. No, her midnight attack was not something that could be brushed aside and forgotten as she got on with her day. Last night, it had sounded like a personal interview with the detective in charge was on the agenda.

Carina hauled herself out of bed and went to the closed door of the bedroom. Her host must have shut it and left her to sleep while he entertained Jace. Another sign of thoughtfulness from him, but a sign of carelessness on her part—or extreme exhaustion. How had she slept through Jace's awakening? At least another round of giggles assured her that he was in good hands.

She opened the door and peered out into the hallway. No one in sight, but a bathroom beckoned from across the hall. Splashing a little cool water on her face with special attention to her sleep-logged eyes started her on track for the day. She retrieved her toothbrush and hairbrush from her purse and quickly used them. If she had something other than these pajamas to wear, she might start feeling almost normal.

Hadn't Ryder said she might find clothes that would fit her in his mother's closet? But searching through another woman's things was too intrusive. She couldn't do it. Where was Ryder's mother anyway? He was too young for her to have passed away from old age.

There was so much she didn't know about her neighbor. Like why he was no longer a cop. Had he done something that got him fired? The uniformed officer hadn't hinted at such a thing last night. No, she'd mentioned only commendations. Yet the air of tragedy about Ryder was palpable. With her safety and that of her son in his hands, however temporarily, maybe she'd be wise to find out more about him.

On that thought, she headed up the hallway to track down her son and her host. The flooring appeared to be hardwood original with the house, but the finish was unmarred, like it had been recently redone. The soft gray paint on the walls seemed to be fresh also. Someone had been renovating. Ryder had mentioned something about that during their conversation last night.

Carina arrived at a spacious living room furnished in retro modern décor to find Jace stuffing Cheerios in his mouth from among dozens of pieces strewn across a glass-topped coffee table. Ryder sat cross-legged on a sectional, dressed in a fresh pair of jeans and a loose-fitting T-shirt. A mug of what might be coffee rested next to him on a side table, and Jace's diaper bag was perched at his feet.

The man was grinning at the toddler who was enjoying his breakfast. She'd judged Ryder to be in his midthirties, but the smile turned the calendar back a few years.

At her appearance, both heads swiveled her way.

"Ma-ma!" Jace squealed and chugged toward her on chubby legs, still clad in last night's pajamas, just like his mother.

Carina scooped him up and he patted her cheeks with the palms of his plump little hands. Surprisingly, his bottom felt dry. She'd expected to find him sodden after his hours of sleep. She looked to her host, who had risen from his seat.

"You change diapers?"

"I'm a pro at peekaboo, too." His grin reappeared and her heart did an absurd jig. "My sister has two kids, one of them not much older than Jace. I learned fast."

Carina locked gazes with her son. "Are you having fun with our neighbor, Mr. Jameson?"

"Too late for formalities," said her host. "I've already taught him to call me Ryder."

"I'der… I'der," chanted her son.

She laughed. "I guess you've discovered Jace has an outgoing personality. From a mother's perspective, he's fearless. He's never gone through a phase of being shy with strangers."

"I was a bit surprised when he trotted in here on his own and didn't bat an eyelash when I picked him up."

Carina sobered. "I'm so sorry I slept late and left you with his care."

"No problem. Your little guy is one hundred percent a genuine pleasure to be around."

"We are most definitely agreed on that point."

They shared a laugh, and their gazes met. Was that a spark of beyond-casual interest she glimpsed in his eyes? Surely not. Her imagination must be working overtime because of raw emotions.

His attention fell away as his head abruptly turned toward the front door. The doorbell rang and her body gave an involuntary jerk. Judging by his alert response, Ryder must have heard an approach even before the bell rang.

"I'll get it." He lifted an admonishing finger. "Step out of sight into the dining room."

Heart bobbing in her chest like a buoy in a rough sea, she clutched Jace close and quickly obeyed. Did he really think an assailant would ring the doorbell? Probably not. But he wasn't taking any risks either, and that was a level of caution she could appreciate.

Fingers of one hand wrapped around the grip of the Smith & Wesson 9 mm concealed in the pancake holster at his waist, Ryder trod to the door and peered out through the peephole. The female officer from last night stood on his porch. Releasing a pent-up breath, he opened the door to her.

"Good morning, sir," she said with a tired grimace that tried to masquerade as a smile. "I'm returning your shotgun. It's been checked out and, just as you said in your statement, it hasn't been fired. We have no need to keep it for evidence."

"Thank you." Ryder accepted the firearm from her. "How are the CSIs doing over at Carina's house?"

"They're done, actually. She can go home now. But Detective Worthing would like to see both of you at the station as soon as you can make it."

"We'll be there." Carina's voice came from a few paces behind Ryder.

He turned to find her standing behind him, holding Jace. The little boy's bright, curious eyes studied the officer's uniform with its shiny trappings.

"Sounds good. I'll leave you then," the officer said. The wave she offered was returned by Jace. "Cute kid." An easier smile than the first attempt brightened her face.

Ryder's heart squeezed. If his understanding was correct, brothers in blue had been badly injured last night by this lowlife professional killer who'd attacked Carina. The whole force would be battling a toxic emotional cocktail of grief, outrage, and frustration, making genuine smiles difficult. Leave it to a tot to help lighten the mood a bit.

The officer left and Ryder turned to his

guests. "I can drive us to the station whenever you're ready."

Carina opened her mouth but no words came out. Then she shook her head. "I'll drive."

Ryder's gut went a little hollow. What was the matter with him that he was looking forward to spending more time with this pair, even if it *was* on a short trek to a police interview? Of course, there was also the matter of their safety with a killer on the loose. But then, who had made him their bodyguard? Himself, that's who. But he needed Carina's cooperation if that informal arrangement was to work.

"At least let me follow you," he said.

She lifted a hand. "No, I didn't mean we had to go separately. Just that I'll be the driver. Jace's car seat is in my SUV, and it's a pain to move it from vehicle to vehicle."

Ryder's heart lightened. "Good call. I hadn't thought of that."

"I want to go home now and take a shower and get both Jace and myself into clean clothes. Give me your phone number and I'll call you when we're ready to go."

Clearly, he wasn't invited along on the cleanup expedition, but she should be safe enough in broad daylight when the cops had barely vacated the premises.

Ryder swiped his phone off his belt next to

the gun. "Tell you what. Give me your number and I'll call you with it right now. Then you'll have mine."

They performed the number exchange and a minute later, he waved as she and Jace headed up the sidewalk toward home. He waited and watched until they disappeared inside the house.

Time to do a little cleanup of his own. With his newly met neighbors in mind, he'd taken a hard look in the mirror when he got up this morning. How had he allowed himself to become such a scraggly specimen? The old Ryder Jameson had been as clean-cut as they came. But that was the problem. He wasn't the old Ryder anymore, and he didn't yet know what the new guy would become.

As he took scissors and then a razor to the bristles on his face, gut-punching images attacked him.

He and his SWAT partner Ron hustled in formation into the warehouse, intent on rounding up the human trafficking ring and liberating a shipment of kidnapped women. But contrary to all intelligence and their own eyes, which had witnessed suspects going inside, the building appeared vacant. Just a bunch of crates and rusting machinery.

Then they saw it. The bomb. No timer. A re-mote-controlled detonator that could be trig-gered at any moment.

Ron whirled on him. Rushed at him. Pressed him toward the exit. Were they going to get out in time?

A brilliant blast and everything—includ-ing himself—tumbled through the air, as if in a pressure vacuum. He was both blinded and deafened by the explosion.

Then—who knew how long after—he pulled his broken body into a sitting position amid the rubble. His ears still rang but his sight was fully engaged. Sickening carnage—what was left of people he knew and cared about. There was no remedy for reality. He was the only survivor.

A strange sound filled Ryder's bathroom—something between a growl and a whine. He opened eyes he hadn't realized he'd jammed shut. The noise was coming from his own throat. A white-knuckled fist clenched the razor he'd been wielding. Dropping the razor into the sink, he willed the awful keening to stop rising out of his chest then hauled a deep breath of oxygen into his lungs.

The flashbacks hadn't gotten any less in-tense, though the docs had assured him they would. They had, however, become less frequent. He'd take any small mercy he could get. Like the fact that the perpetrators of the bombing had been caught and incarcerated while he'd been engaged in the lengthy recovery from his injuries. Justice helped. Justice was right. But it didn't bring any of his friends and colleagues back, and so the grief and guilt continued.

The ringtone on his cell began to play. He picked up his phone, which he'd kept close on the bathroom shelf. It was Carina.

"That was fast," he said. Did his voice quaver? Probably. Hopefully, she wouldn't notice.

A soft chuckle answered. The pleasant sound rippled through him, loosening tense muscles in his chest.

"One learns to shower quickly with an infant in the house. I have to put him in his play yard, where he doesn't want to be, while I take care of myself. My shower was accompanied by angry howling."

"I could have looked after him here."

There was slight hesitation then a clearing of the throat. "Certainly, but you've been more than gracious in that regard. Anyway, I also needed to freshen him up and change his clothes."

Ryder could respect her desire not to depend on a near stranger, but she might not have much choice when a killer was out there with her name on his hit list.

"I'll be over in a jiffy. Don't step foot outside until I'm with you."

A sharp intake of breath. "Why are you doing this?"

"Scaring you with my instructions?"

"No, risking yourself for neighbors you've just met."

He'd asked himself why he was set on doing this, too, but something in him said there was no other course of action. "How can I do anything else? Besides, I've gotten in this guy's way once, and he wasn't happy about it. Who knows if I'm not in his sights now as well?"

"I can't believe this is happening. Why?"

Did she truly not have a clue about the motive behind the attempt on her life? She seemed sincere when she said it, but "cop think" had trained him not to accept much at face value. Maybe she knew something she didn't see as relevant.

"Let's get down to the police station," he said, "and do what we can to help the cops find answers."

"You're right." A brief catch of breath. Was she choking back well-warranted tears? "I'll be here waiting for you." Her voice came out thin and high.

Tears, for sure.

"I'm on my way."

If only he could promise her everything was going to be all right. But he knew too well that sometimes the good guys lost.

Not today, if he could help it.

Ryder strode to his bedroom and opened his gun safe. He deposited his shotgun inside and removed his SIG-Sauer P320. It wasn't his service weapon. He'd had to give that up when he left the department, but it was an identical make and model, more comfortable in his hand even than the lighter weight Shield at his waist. It also held more rounds. He donned his shoulder holster and made sure he had extra mags of ammo for both handguns he was carrying.

Overkill? Maybe. No pun intended. But they were dealing with a guy so clever that he escaped police custody, and so ruthless he hadn't balked at sending officers to the hospital in the process.

A minute later, Ryder arrived on Carina's doorstep and she let him in. Jace was wrapped in one of her arms, diaper bag and purse slung over the other arm. Must be staples of her life with a small child. The toddler grinned at him and clapped his hands. Ryder grinned back.

Nice to be popular. They'd become pretty good friends over Cheerios and a game of peekaboo.

Carina's eyebrows lifted as she studied his newly shaven face. What did she think? Her expression didn't give away much. Then her glance fell to the gun in his shoulder holster. His smaller pistol was hidden under the T-shirt that extended below his belt. Her lips thinned, but she made no remark about either his altered appearance or the state of his armament.

"We can go out through the kitchen," she said. "My vehicle is in the attached garage. While we're out and about, would you like to help me shop for a security system for the house?"

"Good idea," he said as they wove around the stacks of moving boxes toward the entrance to the garage. Traces of CSI activity showed here and there, evidenced by dark fingerprint powder. "Do you want to swing by a drive-through for a bit of breakfast before we go to the police station? I know you can't have had time to eat."

She shook her head. "My stomach is twisted in knots. I don't think I could choke anything down."

They entered a one-stall garage lined with moving boxes, leaving just enough space for a compact SUV. Lingering odors of motor oil and some sort of shellac or paint had to be legacies of a prior tenant.

Carina began buckling Jace into his car seat, which was turning into a bit of a challenge as the little guy wriggled and grabbed at the zoo animal mobile dangling from the carrier handle.

"I hope you don't find me nosy," she said as she straightened from the chore and met his gaze. "You said I was in your mother's room. Is she on vacation or something?"

Ryder's jaw tensed, but at least she wasn't asking why he was no longer a cop.

He forced a smile and shook his head. "Not on vacation. It's a bit of a long story. I'll give you the nutshell version on the way."

They climbed into the vehicle, with her behind the wheel, and then pulled out onto the quiet, residential street.

Ryder's gaze roamed the area, assessing for threats. "Dad was killed in a car accident five years ago, and Mom's in a care facility." The simple, devastating truth was dust in his mouth.

"Oh, that's awful. I'm sorry." She glanced his way, eyes shadowed. "Was your mom in the accident, too? Is that why she's in care?"

Ryder shook his head. "She was diagnosed with multiple sclerosis a decade back, but about two years ago, she finally got to where she couldn't look after herself anymore."

"Must be hard for your family."

"My sister and I are struggling more with it than Mom seems to be." Ryder let out a brief chuckle. "She's the most cheerful person I know. The staff at the care center call her their ray of sunshine. Mom can't even feed herself, but she brightens the life of everyone who comes into contact with her. Jesus is her best friend, and she lets everyone know it."

"My kind of woman." Carina grinned. "She sounds amazing."

"She is. If you want, maybe I'll introduce you sometime."

Ryder resisted an impulse to literally bite his tongue. Why had those words popped out of his mouth? Years as a cop had trained impulsive speaking out of him. Or so he'd thought. Something about this woman got under his skin. Maybe the sweet innocence of her little son had transferred sweet innocence to Carina. There *could* be a reason for the attempt on her life that implicated her in criminal activity. But he didn't think so. He was very good—some people called him uncanny—at detecting signs of lying or holding back in people. He hadn't picked up on any of those signals in her. However, as long as a killer was after her, he wasn't taking her anywhere near his mother.

Carina gave him a sidelong look, probably wondering what to make of the suggestion coming from a near stranger bonded with her by crisis alone.

But then her expression smoothed. "I think I'd like that."

They continued chatting about his mother, a surprisingly pleasant topic, as they made their way to the police station. Since Carina was unfamiliar with the layout of Argyle, Ryder interjected their discussion with directions on which way to go. The station was on the other side of town, reached from this location partly on single-lane roads and partly on the two-lane state highway that ran through the middle of the town. Halfway into the journey and after the third turn, he was certain of what he'd started to suspect a few minutes ago.

Ryder shot Carina a grim frown. "We've got a tail."

THREE

They were being followed? Carina's pulse performed a tap dance in her throat. Her gaze flitted from her rearview mirror to her side-view one. No vehicle stood out to her in the moderate traffic.

"Are you sure?"

"Dark blue sedan three cars back."

Another glance in her rearview showed her the vehicle. "I see it," she said.

"They've made every turn with us, smooth as glass, and not following too closely."

"Professional?"

He rolled his shoulders. "Not a rookie."

Carina's fingers clenched around the steering wheel. Was she supposed to engage in some sort of evasive maneuvers? The idea sent her heart racing. She *was* a rookie at anything like that.

"What should I do?" Her words came out like she was a little short of breath.

"Not a thing," he said. "Proceed to the police station like we haven't got a care in the world."

Carina shot him a sideways glance. Not a care? Who was he kidding?

He sent her a grin that lacked humor. "If they're up to no good, somewhere close to the cop shop is the last place they'll try anything."

"Right." She allowed herself a full breath.

Another mirror check revealed the sedan was still behind them. She pressed on the gas and increased her speed as high as she dared within city limits. Ryder offered her a nod then returned his eyes to the passenger's-side mirror.

"I'll let the local PD know we're bringing company." He took out his phone and tapped in a number.

To whoever answered, Ryder quickly summarized the situation while craning his neck this way and that between the passenger's-side mirror and the rearview one he'd hijacked from Carina.

"I've got a bad angle to see the full license plate," he told the person on the other end of the connection, "but there are a few letters." He rattled them off then paused, angling his head this way and that. "One of the numbers is three. The vehicle is a late-model Chevy, probably an Impala."

He went silent, listening, and then the call was over.

"What did they say?" she blurted.

"They're redirecting a unit, but we'll probably reach the station before they can get to us. They're also opening the gated employee lot for us to pull into rather than risking the open visitor lot."

"Aren't they going to stop the vehicle that's following us and arrest whoever's inside?"

"As soon as we're safe, they'll pull them over. As to an arrest, it depends on the driver's identity and story."

Carina shifted in her seat. "Like there could be an innocent explanation?"

"Not impossible."

"But not probable?"

Ryder's answer was a deep frown and a long stare over his shoulder. "Our tail is making a move. Closing in."

Carina's mouth went dry. "What do I do? We're about to turn onto the state highway, but the light is yellow."

"Gun it!"

She mashed her foot down on the accelerator and swept through the turn even as the light went red. Angry horns blared, but not at them. She hadn't obstructed traffic.

"Our pursuer blew the red?" she asked.

"You got it. Bearing down fast." He pulled the gun from his shoulder holster. "Whatever happens, keep driving toward the station. But drive safe."

"Precious cargo," Carina bit out between clenched teeth.

"For sure."

Jace seemed oblivious to the tension swirling around him. He was chortling in the back seat, no doubt making his mobile animals dance.

A sharp *snick* sent tingles down Carina's spine. Ryder had racked a bullet into the chamber of his pistol.

Please, God, no shooting with Jace in the car.

"I'm going to try to get us out of this with no gunfire, but it's best to be prepared." Ryder's thoughts must be paralleling hers. "Stay in the right lane. Steady now, but be ready to make a sharp turn when I give the word."

Carina's stomach roiled. The blue sedan was creeping nearer, and it had moved to the next lane over. Soon it would pull alongside their SUV. The enemy vehicle drew close enough for her to see in through the front window. A driver alone. If the driver was armed, it would be difficult for the person to shoot and control a vehicle at the same time. How was that a threat? Maybe they'd misread the situation.

Or maybe they hadn't. Her heart skipped a beat. The sedan was inching alongside them, near enough now to make out the driver's face from the side-view mirror. Only there was no face. The driver wore a grinning gorilla mask. Terror clawed its way up Carina's throat. She stomped on the gas and the steering wheel went wobbly in her grip.

"Whoa!" Ryder grabbed the wheel, steadying the vehicle.

Carina heaved in a breath. "Sorry, the guy's wearing a mask. I've had a phobia about those since childhood." She swallowed against the tightness in her throat.

Now was not the time to get into her kidnapping experience. She didn't actually *remember* her kidnapper wearing a mask, but he must have because she'd been left with an irrational terror of masks ever since.

The other car crept close again and the driver's right hand lifted to reveal something bulky gripped in its fist.

A chill squeezed Carina's insides. "I think he's got a gun!"

"Turn! Now!"

At Ryder's command, Carina whipped the steering wheel to the right, and they tore at street speed into the large parking lot of the local grocery store. Centrifugal force threw her against the door, but her seat belt prevented any real impact. Jace let out a startled squawk.

"Keep going," Ryder said, voice low and intense.

"Did the other guy make the turn?"

"Nope. But he saw what direction we're headed. Don't slow down. Skirt the edge of the lot to avoid pedestrians. Then at the back exit take a quick left. That road leads directly toward the station."

"Maybe he knows that's where we're going."

"He's got an educated guess, I'd imagine, the morning after a felony attack."

How could Ryder sound so cool and calm?

"He could try to intercept us." Her tone came out a husky whisper as she whipped the vehicle onto the street behind the grocery store. Good thing there was little traffic on this side road.

"He might try that," Ryder said, "but he'd be wiser to back off. We're within blocks of the station."

Inhaling breaths in shallow gulps, Carina navigated toward safety. Every detail of her surroundings leaped out at her. Is this what was called hypervigilance induced by danger? Whatever it was, she barely slowed as she turned in at the gates of the station's fenced squad car lot. Then she slammed on the brakes and brought the SUV to a rocking halt, knuckles white.

Ryder's big, warm hand closed around one of hers. "It's okay now. You did great. We made it, and here comes the cavalry."

Half a dozen officers swarmed her SUV.

Carina dropped her sweat-beaded forehead onto the coolness of the steering wheel and burst into tears. She turned her hand and gripped Ryder's, probably crushing his fingers, but a tight hold on someone was a thing she needed right now. His steady, kind voice kept assuring her they were safe. With several gasps, she seized control of herself and sat up, releasing his hand.

"I'm sorry about that." Carina wiped at the wetness on her cheeks.

"Totally understandable."

A knock on her driver's-side window sent a tremor through her body and brought her head around. A short, lanky, middle-aged man with close-cropped, salt-and-pepper hair and distinct wrinkle lines bracketing his mouth stood gazing at her with shrewd chocolate-brown eyes.

"Let's get you folks inside," he said.

Carina's hand shook as she unlatched the door, but she steeled herself and got out.

"Detective David Worthing," the man said, extending his hand.

She took it and found it paper-dry and bony. Hers probably felt like a wet noodle to him.

"Let me get my son out of the car and then—"

She turned around to find Ryder behind her, holding Jace in his arms. Looking none the worse for wear, her little guy gazed around at the people and vehicles in the lot. Carina dredged up a smile for him and he reached for her. She took Jace from Ryder and wrapped him close in both arms, inhaling the sweet, baby scent of her little boy.

What if he'd been hurt because someone was after his mommy? The thought terrified her more than death itself. But what could she do to ensure nothing like that happened?

Ryder followed Carina and Jace as the detective led the way through the service door of the building. The uniformed officers formed a rear guard. They went along a scuffed linoleum-floored hallway, with offices to the right and left, and then emerged into a larger room. Ryder's steps slowed. Here was the bullpen where the rank and file sat around cheap desks, drank bad coffee and—yes, there was the evidence on one of the desks—ate doughnuts. Some stereotypes were more true than false.

He inhaled deeply of the familiar odors and his heart squeezed. A part of him missed this very much. Just not a big enough part to entice him back into the fray. Not yet anyway. Maybe not ever. His next direction in life was something he needed to figure out—as soon as he was sure Carina and Jace were safe. For that to happen, the real threat needed to be exposed and arrests needed to be made.

As the detective led them through the bullpen and into a small conference room, Ryder's hands balled into fists. Certain lowlifes who accosted people in their homes and terrorized them on the road needed to be caught right now!

"The unit you sent our way had to have been getting close," Ryder said as they took seats at the scarred wooden table. "Were they able to make the stop? Is the driver of that blue sedan in custody?"

The detective gazed at them soberly and let out a sigh.

"I'll take that as a no," Ryder said.

Next to him, Carina made a sound like a soft squeak. Dire frustration. She must be frantic for news that signaled this nightmare coming to an end, and she had yet to receive it.

Worthing leaned toward them. "We found the vehicle that matched the description in a pharmacy parking lot, but it was empty. We identified it as reported stolen sometime last night. The vehicle is being examined for evidence as we speak."

"He was wearing a gorilla mask," Carina blurted out. "As if this is all fun and games for him."

"You're sure the driver was male?" Worthing asked.

She opened her mouth then shut it and huffed a long breath. "I had that impression, but no, I'm not certain."

"Carina had a better look at who was behind the wheel than I did," Ryder said. "The set of the shoulders appeared masculine. But can we confirm the driver was the same man from last night? No."

"You mean it could have been someone other than the man who attacked me in my home?" Eyes wide, Carina stared at him. "How many people are out to kill me?"

"One," Ryder answered. "At least, it's my

working theory that an individual has hired one or more people to do their dirty work."

"That's our working theory, too," Worthing said. "Especially after we ran the prints from the man who broke into your house."

Carina gaped at the detective. "But the guy was wearing gloves, and he got away before he could be brought to the station."

"The gloves were removed when he was cuffed," Ryder told her. "He would have left prints in the squad car."

"And DNA in both the seized gloves and the car," the detective added. "The DNA result is pending, but the prints are a match for a known contract killer."

Carina sat back. Jace began to fuss and she bounced him automatically. "Does this man have a name? For some reason, if I have an identity, he might seem less of an inhuman monster to me."

Worthing's thin lips curled in a sneer. "He's human all right, but cold-blooded as they come. And this guy isn't known by a name or a face, just a reputation. Last night was the first time his face has been seen by a victim who lived to tell about it. He's never been in police custody, but he's wanted internationally."

Ryder groaned and scrubbed a hand over his face. "And we lost him."

"*We* did, for the moment." Worthing sent him a long look and a tiny, knowing grin.

Ryder's face heated. Reflex to think of himself as a cop, and Worthing well knew it. Another symptom that he wasn't doing a very good job of moving on with his life.

"But now we have something we've never had before on last night's contract killer," the detective went on. "A solid description of him. Up until now, we've known of his existence and basic MO, but we haven't had so much as a name or a face to put to him. I'd like each of you to sit with a forensic artist I've called in and help her draw up a likeness of this guy."

Carina stood, still bouncing an increasingly fussy baby. "No art for me until this little man is changed, fed and down for a nap, in that order."

"Of course." Worthing smiled. "I'll get one of the duty officers to take you somewhere private where you can see to his needs."

Moments later, Carina rose to follow a junior officer out of the room. At the door, she stopped and looked back over her shoulder.

"I'm being very self-centered," she said. "How are your men in the hospital?"

Worthing's regard darkened. "Critical. We don't know yet if they'll make it."

"I'm so sorry." Moisture shimmered in her eyes.

"Me, too. Thank you for asking."

Ryder sent her an approving smile. Self-centered? Hardly. Considering what she was going through, it was a sign of a caring nature that she remembered other people's troubles. Sure, his cop mind was trying to look at every angle, including the possibility that something criminal in her background might have put her in the crosshairs, but his gut was telling him she was exactly who she seemed to be—a decent human being and a terrific mother.

And quite gorgeous in a way that appealed to him like no other woman in recent history. But he was a personal mess, and she was *in* a mess, so now was not the time for attraction to be a consideration.

She pulled the door mostly closed and left with her escort, leaving Worthing and Ryder in the little conference room.

Ryder locked gazes with the cool-eyed detective. "I don't believe the person in the car today was the contract killer. Why wear a mask when we saw him last night?"

"Terror factor?" The detective shrugged.

"Does this guy's MO include taunting a mark?"

"No, it doesn't." Worthing leaned closer across the table, as if sharing a confidence. "Hits connected to him have been all business. Fast and clean. So I'm inclined to agree with your suggestion that our gorilla was someone else."

"Perhaps the person who contracted the hit?"

"Could be, but that's getting more speculative." The detective sat back and crossed his arms.

"But if it wasn't, then we have another player in this dirty game."

"True, but we don't have enough information yet to rule that idea out."

"The key to this case is motive." Ryder rubbed the tense muscles in his jaw, a bit surprised to find smooth skin under his fingers. "If we can figure out *why* someone wants Carina dead, then we are likely to know who's behind the attempts. She's consistently denied any knowledge of why anyone would want to kill her. But maybe she knows something about this business that she's either not telling us, for whatever reason, or she doesn't realize it's connected. The smallest thing could be significant."

"Your reputation as a homicide detective precedes you." Worthing shot him a wolfish grin. "How would you like to join the department and help us solve this? Argyle is growing by the day, and we could use another detective."

Ryder's chest constricted. Why did that idea sound tempting to him? He'd abandoned police work. He wanted his life to take a fresh direction. Didn't he? Besides, Carina and Jace needed a protector as much as they needed a detective.

He released the air he'd been hoarding in his lungs and shook his head. "Not at this time. Police departments aren't set up to provide round-the-clock protection for any single citizen. Right now, my time is at my discretion."

"And you want to use it to watch over Jace and Carina." Worthing gave him a tight-lipped stare. "Are you sure that urge has nothing to do with the fact that she's pretty and he's cute?"

"Of course not!" The denial came out a little too strong, even to his own ears.

Was that amusement dancing in the detective's gaze?

"What I mean is—" Ryder moderated his tone "—yes, she's pretty and he's cute, but I've seen enough death. As a homicide detective, I was always on the scene after the fact. Maybe this time I'm in a position to get in front of a tragedy and prevent it from happening. If, in the process, we find out that Carina knows something or did something with criminal implications, so be it, but at least her kid won't be an orphan."

"Fair logic." Worthing nodded. "And if you stay close to her, and she trusts you, maybe you'll find out what she knows and can pass that information along."

A sour taste invaded Ryder's mouth. "I've gone from detective to informant now?"

"Sounds like that's a necessary part of the role you're choosing."

"There's also the possibility that Carina is entirely innocent in all this."

"I hope that's the case, but we still need to uncover the reason she's a target."

Ryder leaned an elbow on the table and fixed the detective with a stare. "I know you've been digging into her background. That's a given. Is there something I should know about her?"

The detective's lips thinned and he went pale. The grim expression set Ryder's teeth on edge. The nature of the problem had to be beyond awful to turn a veteran policeman white.

"Twenty years ago," the man said, his tone a low growl, "Carina's parents were shot to death in their Tulsa home by an unknown assailant, and she was abducted. The police and even the FBI turned over every imaginable rock trying to find her, but it was as if she vanished without a trace. Whoever killed her parents and took her left nothing behind in the way of clues. Her family's lives were examined under a microscope, but no skeletons popped out that would suggest a motive or a perpetrator."

Ryder gulped down a lump in his throat. Carina had been through the wringer, all right. And he thought *he'd* been served a bad dish!

"But, clearly, she was eventually found," he said.

Worthing shook his head. "Not by law enforcement. She simply turned up one day a week later, wandering aimlessly through a public park, still dressed in the pajamas she'd been wearing when she was taken. She was hungry, dehydrated and dazed."

A slow burn took up residence in Ryder's gut. "Surely, she was able to give law enforcement valuable information. At least, there would have been forensic evidence on her clothes or body." Someone needed to be held accountable for such vile actions.

"An arrest was never made," Worthing said. "In fact, no viable suspects were ever identified. She remembered hiding in terror in her bedroom closet from an intruder, but had no memory of what took place between her disappearance and her reappearance. Forensics made little headway."

"Was she physically harmed?" His question came out thin through a constricted throat.

"No, but a cocktail of drugs was found in her system."

"Explaining the lack of memory."

"That would make sense in a kidnapping scenario, but there were traces of drugs in her bloodstream that should have enhanced recollection, not wiped it out. However, a generous mixture of sedatives was also present. The memory loss could be psychological. What ever took place was too terrifying for her mind to handle, so the memories were suppressed."

Ryder's heart wrung. "What happened after she recuperated? The foster system?"

The detective smiled faintly. "That's the one bright spot in the story. She had an aunt who was more than willing to take her in."

"Maybe the abductor is getting nervous she might remember something."

"After this long?" Worthing snorted.

"It's an avenue of inquiry. Could the man who attacked her in her home, the contract killer, be the one who murdered her parents and took her? Maybe we're not looking at a hit for hire."

The detective grimaced. "Nice and neat if it could be played that way, but a partial fingerprint at a crime scene in Philadelphia puts our contractor *there* at the time of the murders and abduction in Tulsa. That hit in Philly is the first record of this guy's activity as a killer for hire, and the last time until now that we have fingerprint evidence."

"The man's had a long career then. Twenty years and never been caught, much less identified?"

"That's why the FBI is waiting with bated breath for the sketches you and Carina are going to give us. If there's any indication the guy is hanging around to try again, you can be sure we'll have special agents on our doorstep to put her under surveillance twenty-four-seven."

A small sound drew Ryder's attention to the doorway. Carina stood just over the threshold, sans baby, scowling like she was about to rain down thunder and lightning.

"That's your brilliant plan? Use me as bait to catch a killer?" Her face flushed bright red. "Why don't you concentrate on finding who hired him, and get Jace and me out of danger before worrying about catching an international hit man? With that kind of thinking, how can I have any confidence law enforcement will find the person who wants me dead? It'll be just like before. Lots of investigating. No results."

Carina slammed the conference room door and stomped away. The decisive bang echoed in Ryder's ear. She'd asked great questions and looked scary beautiful doing it.

From the cop perspective, he understood the detective's words hadn't been meant the way they'd sounded to her. Cops could be multi-taskers with more than one objective. But from his newly civilian perspective, he agreed that it sounded like the focus of the investigation was too much on catching the contract killer and not enough on discovering who hired him.

Not that it would be a bad thing to have her under continual surveillance by the FBI, but that predicated allowing the killer to try again. Not Ryder's priority at all. Did he need to do some investigating of his own? Tall order, when he was also committed to standing between Jace and Carina and whoever was after her.

FOUR

Carina had read about people experiencing hot and cold flashes in moments of fear, but until this moment, she had attributed the description to exaggeration. Now she was physically living those sensations. A moment ago, she'd felt safe here in the bowels of the police station and, technically, she was. But as soon as she left the premises, law enforcement would be eager for her assailant to try again. Did ex-cop Ryder Jameson feel the same way?

Her stiff-legged steps slowed and then halted at the door to the small office where she had left Jace sleeping on a pile of blankets under the watchful eye of the duty officer. Carina turned the knob and pressed the door open a crack. Jace lay sprawled on his back, sound asleep, exactly as she'd left him, chubby face as profoundly peaceful as only a baby's could be. The officer seated at a desk nearby fluttered her fingers and offered a half smile. Carina dredged up a meager return smile then pulled the door shut.

A tremor shook her and her legs suddenly went weak. Only by leaning back against the wall and hugging herself tightly did she remain upright. That gorilla mask! If someone had meant to terrorize her, they'd chosen the right approach. But such petty evil-mindedness didn't match the cool professionalism of the attempt on her life. *Had* the person in the mask been holding a gun? Now that she thought more carefully, she was less certain the item in the gorilla's hand had been a firearm. But if not, what had been the point of this morning's pursuit? She squeezed her eyes shut and pinched the bridge of her nose between her fingers.

"Carina?"

Ryder's soft baritone brought her eyes open and her head up. Fists clenched, she pushed away from the wall and faced him as he came up the hallway, moving in that nearly soundless prowl of his.

Stopping in front of her, he held up a hand, palm out. "I don't blame you a bit for feeling ready to hit someone."

"But not you." She forced her fingers to uncurl. "After all you've done for Jace and me, you don't deserve my anger. I'm being absurd and unfair. The police are doing the best they can in a complicated situation."

"You're also doing the best you can." A mild grin softened his chiseled features. "And your best is turning out to be a whole lot better than lots of folks I've dealt with."

Carina let out a short sniff. "In your former line of work, I'm sure you dealt with plenty of people on the ragged edge. So, what next? I go on my merry way until someone comes after me again and hope the cops are there to grab him before he succeeds?"

Ryder shook his head. "First, we do what we came here to do. That is, give law enforcement all the information we can, so they have everything possible to work with. Then a unit will escort us as we go buy that security system we talked about. The officers will follow us to your house, where you and I will install it together. And somewhere in the mix, we'll grab a bite to eat."

"I'm hearing a lot of 'us' and 'we' in there. You don't have to do any of this. You—"

A sturdy finger gently laid across her mouth halted her flood of objections.

"If you had caught a little more of my conversation with Detective Worthing," he said, "you would have heard me tell him I can't sit this one out, but I don't want to do it like a cop, arriving on the scene *after* the worst has happened. This is my opportunity to get out in front of something and do whatever I can to stop it."

Carina planted her hands on her hips. "You've already done that once, and I'm deeply grateful, but Jace and I don't need to be made into someone's project."

Ryder's expression tightened. "That's not at all what I meant. I'm already involved. Backing off now is not an option."

She opened her mouth, further objections on her tongue. This man had gone above and beyond what anyone could expect. She should insist he get on with his life. He wasn't responsible for her. She didn't *want* anyone to be responsible for her. Then she closed her mouth with a snap. With the events of last night, all hope of her prized independence had melted away like a mirage. She would be a great fool to reject any help she could get—not only for herself, but for the sake of the little life depending on her.

"All right then." She nodded. "I guess I can handle the baby steps you've outlined."

His face relaxed. "If we manage all that today, we'll have made great strides."

Carina inhaled a deep breath and let it out slowly. "I don't know how I can possibly sleep tonight." She dropped her gaze and bit her lip. How pitiful she sounded.

"You and Little Bit will be under surveillance by the good guys every minute."

"Including you, I take it."

"Count on it."

If the intensity of his tone and the steadiness of his stare could guarantee Carina's survival, she'd skip with that promise all the way to the bank. A little of the tension ebbed from her gut.

"Ryder. Carina." Detective Worthing's voice came from up the hallway. "The sketch artist is here."

"Let's get to it, then," Carina answered. "Before Jace wakes up."

Just short of an hour later, they finished with the artist. Ryder's and her description of the assailant dovetailed in every aspect that mattered. She might have given the guy a bit wider mouth and he a slightly longer nose, but they were in accord with a compromise that left them and the sketch artist with reasonable confidence they had captured the man's likeness in a manner that would render him visually identifiable.

As they were finishing up, Worthing stepped

to the workstation they had been using and took a look at the result.

The man let out a soft hum followed by a grin. "The feds are going to throw a party. I wouldn't be surprised if this lowlife's mug goes viral throughout global law enforcement within the next twenty-four to forty-eight hours. Finally knowing what he looks like will be a big help in apprehending him. Good work." He slapped Ryder on the back and offered Carina a brisk nod.

The former gazed at the detective with a downward quirk to his lips. "And *I* wouldn't be surprised if the guy decides sudden retirement in some hidey-hole off the grid is in his own best interests."

Carina gasped and touched Ryder's arm. "If the professional goes into hiding, and what's left is some creep who gets his jollies out of scaring people by wearing masks, maybe it will be a little while before my unknown enemy can reorganize for another serious attempt. That's good for us, isn't it?"

"I'm cautiously optimistic that will be the case." He smiled at her, his whole face lighting up.

The oxygen vacated her lungs. What was the matter with her? She'd never been the type to go gooey over a guy—not even as a teenager.

Not even when she'd met and married Dillon. Their relationship had been heartfelt, but solid, steady and dependable. Exactly what she'd been looking for.

Ryder rose from his chair and stretched his arms with a groan. Carina wrenched her gaze from him. Attractive didn't begin to describe this guy, but no way could she allow herself to notice. Her response to him had to be some sort of aberration brought on by the intensity of the situation. That was her story and she was sticking to it. But at least, in all fairness, she could acknowledge her initial assessment of him as Mr. Scruffy no longer stood.

Carina's stomach made a low grumbly noise and her face heated. "Jace should be waking up any minute now. How about we detour through a drive-through on our way to doing our errands?"

Ryder patted his flat stomach. "I'm on board with that plan a hundred and ten percent."

Noon had come and gone before Carina pulled her SUV into the garage of her rental house. But their bellies were full of burritos and a state-of-the-art home security system was tucked into the trunk. The marked police car on their tail pulled into the driveway behind them.

"Give your house key to one of the officers,"

Ryder told her. "They'll go in first and make sure it's all clear."

Carina blew out a long breath. "This whole bodyguard thing feels so strange."

Even more restrictive than growing up under the militantly protective scrutiny of Aunt Althea, but Carina wasn't about to mention such a personal detail. The words would make her sound ungrateful to both her dear, well-meaning aunt and her equally well-meaning police protective detail.

Ryder shot her a wry grimace. "Not the sort of thing a person wants to live with indefinitely."

Carina let out a small laugh. "I don't know how celebrities do it. But then—" she sobered "—they're not generally under active threat."

"You continue to impress me with your grasp of situations." He opened his door and climbed out, motioning to the uniforms in the police car.

While the officers checked out the house, Carina got Jace out of his car seat and gathered up the ever-present paraphernalia that came with babies. Ryder collected the packages from the trunk. The officers were shortly back to tell them it was safe to go inside. Carina didn't waste any time taking them up on the invitation.

The cool, dim interior smelled of old wood-work and new packing material. She let out a soft groan as she took in the stacks of boxes and plastic crates yet to be unloaded. That, on top of installing the security system.

"And what about my job?"

"What did you say?" Ryder asked.

His voice jerked Carina out of her over-whelmed funk. She hadn't realized she'd mur-mured her concern aloud.

She turned toward him as he laid the se-curity system packages on the dining room table. "I'm supposed to start as the accountant at Agri-Fresh next week. How is that possibly going to happen now?"

"Agri-Fresh? The farmers' co-op?"

"That's right. The job brought me here."

Ryder rubbed his chin. "That's another pos-sible avenue of inquiry."

"What?" Jace squirmed to be let down. She set him on his feet in front of the large tub of his toys she'd opened for him last night.

"I don't see how yet, but could this new job have anything to do with the attacks on you?"

Carina gaped at him. "Are you serious? I mean, I know money is often the motivation behind crime, but I haven't even begun to crunch any numbers yet."

"Maybe somebody doesn't want to let you."

He forestalled her response with a raised hand. "Like I said, it's simply an avenue of inquiry. Sending a professional hit man after you does seem like an extreme method of stopping you from looking at the co-op's books, especially since they'll only hire someone else if you don't show up. But then, could someone be that desperate?"

"Yikes! Even asking my new boss questions with those kinds of implications could get me fired before I start." She forestalled *his* response the same way he'd done hers. "But then, I'd rather be alive and jobless than employed until I go six feet under."

Ryder smiled. "Good attitude. We'll look into this possibility later. Let me get the security system installed while you look after Jace and do whatever amount of unpacking he allows you to accomplish."

"Once again, you display a sound grasp of the realities of dealing with a toddler." Carina laughed as she narrowly prevented Jace from crawling on top of a box labeled "Fragile."

The jangle of the doorbell stopped the breath in Carina's lungs. Her gaze flew to the front door. This morning the bell at Ryder's house had meant a cop on the front step.

"One of the officers?" She turned toward Ryder.

He shook his head, lips compressed. "They've gone back on patrol. The plan is to station a unit outside after dark when the likelihood of another attempt goes up exponentially. Until then, you're in my hands. Let me handle whoever's at the door, okay?"

Wordlessly, Carina nodded. Surely they were being melodramatic. A contract killer didn't walk up to someone's front door and ring the bell. Did they?

"It's probably an innocent caller," he said as if hearing her thoughts while he moved with a soft tread toward the front window that offered a view of the doorstep. "Maybe a traveling sales rep?" He threw her a smile over his shoulder as he stopped by the curtain. He drew the fabric aside a few inches and his whole body went stiff. "Unbelievable," he muttered, a snarl in his voice. "How did they catch wind of this business? And so quickly?"

Carina's stomach twisted. "Who is it?"

He was shaking his head. "A reporter. There's a news truck idling at the curb."

Carina gasped. Her mouth went stone dry. With a juicy story about a woman attacked in her home at night by a professional hit man who'd also sent cops to the hospital, the media would go into a frenzy. They'd dig up everything about her. What could be as bad as having someone try to kill her? Someone dredging up—for public enjoyment—every painful secret of a past she couldn't fully remember and only wanted to completely forget.

Ryder let the curtain fall back into place, insulating them from the outside world. He turned toward Carina, and his breath caught. She'd gone stone-still, her cheeks white-washed, her gaze faraway and fixed.

He cleared his throat and she blinked.

"I take it you're not doing an interview." Ryder kept his tone light, despite the heaviness in the pit of his stomach.

Her lips peeled back from straight, white teeth as if she'd tasted something nasty. "Not in this century."

"Then we're not at home." He offered a smile and her stiff posture relaxed marginally.

She looked his way. "What if they keep leaning on that button?"

The doorbell chimed again as if to underscore her words.

Ryder grimaced. "We can't keep them from parking on a public street, but we can ask law enforcement to forbid them access to the property this house stands on." He pulled his cell phone from his pocket and waggled it at her.

"You mean shoo them off as trespassers?"

"You got it."

The edges of her mouth tilted slightly upward, but then she suddenly slumped and her
eyes fell away from his.

"Doesn't that make us more or less prison-
ers here? They'll pounce as soon as we step
outside."

"Let's take the problems one at a time."

"Okay." She nodded. "Do it."

Ryder got Detective Worthing on the phone
while Carina turned away and opened one of
the moving boxes. Jace was playing with a
toy truck on the floor at her feet. His engine
noises, including a lot of bubble-blowing and
sputtering, provided a light, innocent background to Ryder's conversation.

"One eviction coming up," he said to Carina
as he ended the call.

She turned from where she was inserting
dishes into a china cabinet set against the wall.
"Thank you. You have no idea what a nightmare it would be for me to be dragged into
the public eye…" She hesitated on a sucked-
in breath. "Again."

Ryder tensed. How badly would she take it
that he already knew the dark circumstances
from her childhood?

"Detective Worthing told you, didn't he?"

Her tone was soft and resigned, not harsh and angry.

"Just the bare facts. I asked if there was anything I needed to know about you."

Carina pressed her lips together and looked away from him. "The kind of facts I suppose anyone could find if they did a little research."

Her eyes darted to the curtained window. Ryder parted the fabric a scant inch. The news truck still idled at the curb, but no reporter stood on the doorstep. The PD officers hadn't had time to get there yet, so no doubt the news personnel were simply biding their time, ready to leap out and close in as soon as anyone attempted to leave the house.

He let out a huff. "I can hardly imagine how distasteful it might be for you to have the old cold case dragged up and rehashed in the media."

"Boggles the mind." She rolled her eyes and attempted a grin that came out more like a grimace. "But that's only the half of it." The muscles around her jawline visibly tensed.

Ryder stepped toward her. "Tell me."

She shrugged and shook her head then went back to placing dishes in the cabinet. Jace was now flying a toy airplane around the room, chortling as he trotted around boxes and swooped the plane to random landings on various containers.

Ryder stopped a few feet from Carina and crossed his arms over his chest. If she had anything to say that impacted the situation they were in, she had better say it.

Carina stopped what she was doing, turned and mirrored his posture. "It's a family thing, all right? Nothing to do with anyone out to kill me. I'm just dreading my aunt hearing about it on the news."

"The aunt who raised you?"

She nodded. "She'll go into a panic."

"Does she have a health condition that would make the shock dangerous for her?"

"Aunt Althea?" Carina's eyes widened. "No, she's healthy as a horse. She'll rush to the rescue, determined to drag me and Jace back to Tulsa where she can watch over us."

"Which could be dangerous for her."

"Absolutely. But she won't see it that way." She flopped her arms against her sides. "And I had a hard enough time wrenching Jace and myself away from her to come here. This situation will start the war for independence all over again." The corners of Carina's mouth drooped. "But I suppose I should get it over with and call her. Better for her to hear something like this from me than a news report."

Carina trod toward her purse, which sat on the table beside the security system packages. A ringtone began to sound from the depths of the bag. She snatched the cell into her hand and her eyes widened. "It's my aunt."

The look she darted at Ryder qualified as deer-in-the-headlights.

He offered her a slight smile. "She may not have heard about this yet."

"Right." Carina huffed. "It would be in character for her to call today to check on us. Here goes." She grimaced and swiped the face of the phone to answer the call.

Ryder went to the table and began unpacking the security system. This conversation was not his business. On the other hand, there might be important knowledge to gain. Whichever was the truth, Carina didn't move away into the other room, and he couldn't help but overhear her end of the conversation. Her words came out measured and weighted, as if she were cautiously maneuvering through a communication minefield—which might be a good analogy in this situation. How did a person tell a loved one about a deadly attack in the night by a professional hit man without alarming them?

Yet, somehow, Carina managed to emphasize the break-in over the shooting part, but it really wasn't possible to minimize the deadly nature of the intrusion. Her aunt's response was loud and staccato, laced with imperatives audible to a bystander, even though the cell's speaker hadn't been activated. The near hysteria Ryder understood, but did a note of eager satisfaction chime through the commands to "come home to me where you belong"?

The hairs on the nape of Ryder's neck stood on end. Was Carina's aunt behind the attack? Was the woman bent on scaring her niece back into the fold? That theory melded well with the person in the mask pursuing them on the road this morning, but it didn't fit with a professional hit man who'd clearly meant to carry out a deadly assignment. Perhaps the two incidents were so discordant because they'd been perpetrated by different parties with different objectives in mind.

"I couldn't possibly come anywhere near you until the police get to the bottom of this matter." Carina's tone was strident, almost shrill. She went stiff and pale as the loud response included something about danger to Jace. "I will take whatever steps are necessary to protect *my* child, Aunt Althea." The words were clipped but raw. "I have to go now, but, please…" A long breath heaved from Carina's lungs. "Please don't talk to any reporters if they come around." She must have received reassurance on that matter because her posture softened. "Thank you. I'll be in touch."

Carina ended the call and lifted her gaze toward Ryder. Her golden-brown eyes glistened with unshed tears and his heart turned over. The conversation with her aunt had taken a lot out of her. Should he even mention his sudden suspicion about her nearest and dearest relative? If the circumstances were not so dire, he'd hold his tongue, but tact would have to take a back seat to plain speaking when lives were on the line.

"Is your aunt so determined to bring you back to her house that she might try to scare you into returning?" He asked the question as gently as possible, but Carina winced anyway.

"What does it say about my family dynamic that I can't rule out the possibility? But not with a deadly attack. Aunt Althea may be fearful by nature and overprotective of her loved ones as a result, but she would never, ever, endanger either me or Jace to get her way. That much I know."

"Doesn't rule out the gorilla sighting. Clearly, whoever was wearing that mask is aware of your phobia, and we've got no way of knowing if your aunt called you from Tulsa just now or from your own backyard."

Carina made a face like she'd tasted something sour and then she shook her head. "My aunt is a Christian woman without a mean bone in her body. The gorilla mask was mean."

Ryder nodded. "It was that, all right. So now we've decided we can trust the aunt, should we consider trusting Jace with her until we ensure you're out of danger?"

"No! I couldn't be parted from him." She hissed in a breath and pressed the heel of a hand to her forehead. "But I have to, don't I?" Her eyes met his and her shoulders squared. "I hate the idea with every fiber of my being, but I can't see a way around it. I love my son too much to let him remain anywhere near harm's way."

The devastation in those amber eyes tore a hole in Ryder's heart even as it heated a furnace in his core. Whatever it took, he *would* get this creep who was trying to harm and terrorize this woman and deprive her little boy of his beautiful mother.

Carina's ringtone began sounding once more, and her lips thinned. "My aunt again, no doubt." Her tone was flat, her posture resigned. "I'll give her the good news that I'm bringing Jace to stay with her."

"*We* are bringing him."

She jerked a nod as her glance dropped to

her cell lying on the table. Her eyes widened. "Not Aunt Althea. The screen says '*Number Unavailable*.'"

"Must be Detective Worthing. You gave him your contact information."

"Oh, right." She picked up her cell.

"Put it on speaker, if you don't mind?"

"You got it." She swiped at the screen and then spoke a quiet hello.

Maniacal laughter answered her. Ice shot up Ryder's spine.

"Ca-ri-na." An eerily distorted bass voice sing songed each syllable. "Don't you know your nightmares will hunt you down?"

FIVE

Carina dropped her cell as if it had burned her and scuttled away from it. Her back met the wall with a dull thump. Blackness edged her vision and roaring filled her ears as her heart ping-ponged around her rib cage. As if viewed from the end of a tunnel, Ryder's large figure stepped into her field of sight, bent and picked up her phone from the floor. His angry voice speaking into it echoed in her head, words and meaning unintelligible in her scrambled brain. Then he plopped the phone onto the table and strode toward her.

Warm arms, strong as steel, wrapped around her and she sagged into them, her face pressed against a sturdy chest. A pleasant woodsy scent filled her nostrils. So, this was what safety felt like.

Safety? Really? A trap, rather. Tempting her to passively leave life and her security in another person's hands. She couldn't do that anymore. No matter what.

Carina stiffened and pulled away from Ryder. His arms fell to his sides. She looked up into his face. His gaze was shadowed, his lips clamped into a pair of taut parallel lines.

"I'm sorry," she breathed. "I've gotten control of myself now. Did the—" Her throat tightened and she swallowed against it. "Did the creep say anything more?"

"Nope. I demanded he identify himself, but he simply disconnected."

"We have to leave. Now! Get Jace to Tulsa and then—"

"We go on the offensive."

Carina blinked up at him. "Go on the offensive how?"

"It's become obvious, hasn't it? What's happening is related to your childhood abduction."

"And the murders of my parents." Each word ripped her heart like tearing a bandage from a wound. Strange how the two-decades-old pain could still be so immediate when there were days she could barely recall her father's and mother's faces.

"I believe solving that cold case will expose who is after you now," Ryder said.

"But it makes no sense to wait twenty years

to try to eliminate me when they released me back when I was a child."

"Do you remember them letting you go?"

Carina lowered her eyes and probed that blank area in her mind. Nothing. Slowly, she shook her head. "No, I have no memory. I'm making an assumption."

"Maybe whoever it was didn't let you go. Maybe you escaped. And maybe something happened to prevent the kidnapper or kidnappers from coming after you at that time."

"Like what?"

Ryder's mouth quirked slightly at the corners. "If we knew the answer to that, we'd be well on the way to solving this mystery."

"If the best effort law enforcement could throw at the case back then couldn't uncover the truth, what makes you think we can solve the crime now?"

"I don't know if we can, but I do know we have to try. No, not we. Me." He poked a thumb at the center of his chest. "You're not eligible for protective custody at this point, but I've got very capable friends who could look after you while I—"

"No, no, no and no." Her tone emerged razor-sharp on every word. "You're a trained investigator. I get that. But you're not official police anymore, so you can't order me out of this. You need me. The information is locked up in here." She tapped the side of her head with her forefinger. "Something we find out in the investigation could break the lock. It's got to. I *have* to remember."

Carina planted her feet and glared up at Ryder. He glared back, jaw twitching.

The sudden crunch and tinkle of shattering glass broke the standoff. Carina's gaze flew toward the sound. Jace had pulled himself on top of the box marked Fragile. Grinning like he was about to conquer Mount Everest, he was attempting to stand up atop it.

With a soft cry, Carina rushed to him then halted short of snatching him off the box. Her son was enjoying a moment of accomplishment. Far be it from her to deny him the fulfillment. By the sound of things, the lamp that was in the box was already broken anyway. She stood close, ready to catch him if he swayed, but Jace stood tall. His face was alight. Giggling, he held out his arms to her, and Carina pulled him close, inhaling the scent she could best describe as innocence and happiness, if such things had an aroma.

Ryder's warm chuckle drew her around to face him.

"You win," he said. "But we *are* going to stash Little Bit with his aunt while we're out sleuthing. And I *am* going to call in a few favors to get Tulsa PD to check in on them regularly."

"Agreed. Won't Detective Worthing back you up with that request?"

"Absolutely. He won't like doing it because we'll be leaving his jurisdiction in the middle of a hot local case, but he can't stop us from going. Then again, a part of him might be a little relieved that we're presumably removing the dangerous parties from the town he's pledged to protect."

"I can understand that perspective in a big-picture sense." She nodded. "What about the FBI?"

Ryder shrugged. "They'll mostly be interested in catching that contract killer. If our drawing doesn't yield quick results, they might want to put you under surveillance, but the feasibility of manpower and expense will make that a short-term arrangement."

"Can they force me into some sort of custody?"

"Nope. Until they're prosecuting a case that requires your testimony, and they have reason to believe your life is in danger because of said testimony, your situation doesn't meet the criteria. And it's not something they can *force* on anyone anyway."

"Will they help us with information about the original investigation of my parents' murders and my abduction?"

Ryder frowned. "Doubtful. I'm technically a civilian now. However—" his understated grin peeked out at her "—I have a few ideas for getting the information through roundabout channels in the Tulsa Police Department. I've got a few favors I can call in."

"What are we waiting for then?"

Something like a vise that had been squeezing her chest let loose and her heart went strangely buoyant. The danger remained omnipresent but doing something proactive was so much better than sitting still, waiting to be attacked.

Ryder glanced at the security system lying half unboxed on the table then shook his head. "No point in wasting time installing that if we're not going to be here."

"I'll go upstairs and pack bags for Jace and me."

"And I'll go next door and grab a few things." He strode to the picture window and parted the curtains. "The television van is still there, but I see a PD cruiser proceeding up the street, so the news crew must have been officially advised to stay off the property. But, so they won't spot me, I'll go out the back door and hustle up the alley. Meet you back here in ten minutes."

Carina laughed. "Make it twenty. If it was just me, I might be able to do ten, but there's a lot to think about when packing for a baby."

"Understandable." He stepped up to her. "Let me borrow your house key so I can let myself back in. I'll return in ten to help you with Jace."

She handed him the key and her eyes followed him out the kitchen door. She bit her lip against an impulse to cry after him to hurry back. He *was* hurrying. Why did she feel so bereft without him right there beside her? Already, she was becoming dependent—a state as dangerous to her mental and emotional health as her physical health was endangered by whoever wanted her dead.

Ryder kept his word and joined her within ten minutes. But even with both of them working on the packing, interspersed with corralling an active toddler, it was half an hour before they were loading Carina's SUV. She buckled Jace into his seat, and Ryder climbed in behind the wheel.

"What about the reporters?" she asked as she slid into the passenger seat. "Won't they follow us?"

"I've got this."

She huffed and buckled her seat belt. At the push of a button, the garage door rumbled upward, and Ryder reversed the car.

Watching over her shoulder, Carina let out a gasp. "The news van backed up to block the driveway."

"No worries."

Her gut clenched as Ryder braked the vehicle mere feet from the side of the news truck. The passenger door opened and a woman began to get out. Was she holding a gun? No, a microphone. A gust of pent-up air left Carina's lungs. So, this wasn't some sort of trick by their enemies masquerading as reporters. The newshounds were playing games trying to get them to stop and talk. That was all.

"Hang on," Ryder called out.

Their vehicle lurched forward and whipped to the right onto the side lawn then performed a full U-turn, bumped over the curb behind the news van and hit the street accelerating. Ryder whooped, Carina laughed and Jace squealed. Not a scared squeal, but an excited sound like he was on a midway ride.

"We'll get well out of town," Ryder said, "and then give Detective Worthing a call to update him."

"He won't be happy."

"He'll be conflicted, but he's really got no

issue with us. We've already given him our best cooperation. If he needs anything more from us, he can give us a call."

A little shudder ran through Carina.

Ryder must have noticed her reaction because he put his hand on her arm. "Don't worry. I'll ask him to use *my* number, not yours, so we won't get blindsided by any more calls from unknown numbers. If the gorilla tries telephone terrorism again, we'll know it's him before we answer."

She gazed toward his sober profile. "Maybe I should change my number."

"And lose an opportunity for him to slip up during the conversation and offer us usable intel?" He glanced her direction, brows drawn together. "If you're game for letting him try to taunt you again."

Carina's stomach roiled. Game? Was she? Not at all. But was she going to let her fear control her? She was not.

"Bring it," she said, fixing her eyes on Ryder. "You know the scariest, most secret thing about me. I hardly know anything at all about you. Well, except you love your mother, Argyle law enforcement seems to respect you and you'll take risks to protect others. Those are good things, and I'm deeply grateful, but that last bit goes with the cop territory. I think it's only right that I should know why I'm sitting next to an ex-cop rather than an active detective."

Color leached from beneath Ryder's healthy tan, leaving his skin waxen. Every inch of him seemed to freeze. Her heart twisted but she didn't withdraw her request for information. What could possibly have been so bad that this courageous, competent man turned to stone at the memory?

Ryder swallowed against a dry throat. He could hardly deny the reasonableness of her need to understand the background of the person who had been thrust into her life under dangerous circumstances. Someone she was now expected to fully rely upon.

But if he'd barely been able to scratch the surface of his trauma in many sessions with the psychiatrist the Oklahoma City PD had provided, how was he going to be able to discuss the worst day of his life with a woman he'd known only since the middle of the night? Besides, all his cop instincts dictated that during a case, information traveled one way—to him, not from him. But this wasn't a case, he wasn't on official duty, and he was no longer a cop—just a guy with a compulsion to protect a woman and a toddler he barely knew.

What was up with that? Atonement for not saving his partner? Or any of his squad? The shrink had worked hard at bringing him around to understand that what had happened wasn't his fault. His head comprehended the fallacy of survivor's guilt, but his heart hadn't gotten the memo yet.

Suck it up, Jameson.

"Started out a routine day on the job." His voice came out a low growl. Not on purpose, but he couldn't force anything more natural past the tension in his neck. "Work the cases, get results. SWAT was an extra gig. Not something I did every day. None of us did. The SWAT unit was only needed on sporadic occasions to address special circumstances. SOP for most police departments."

"SOP?"

"Standard Operating Procedure." Ryder inhaled deeply and shook himself, mentally and physically. *Just give her the facts, man. Just the facts.* How hard could it be? Like a root canal without anesthesia maybe? "Anyway, we got this call-out. A reliable informant had told us that human traffickers we'd been after had a shipment of women held in a certain warehouse. SWAT was tasked to go in there, get them out and apprehend the traffickers, including the big boss we were led to believe would be present. It looked like a major opportunity, but it was a setup. When we breached the warehouse, we found no women, no traffickers, no boss. Only a bomb."

Carina gasped loudly, but Ryder couldn't let her reaction slow him down until he'd spat out the entire mess.

"Our squad leader in front called out that there was no timer on the device, and we'd better evac fast before someone set it off remotely. My partner turned and began running, yelling. I turned, too, and took off, but we were too late."

Ryder's chest cavity cramped and further words died on his tongue. He sat rigid, staring at the road. But his peripheral vision couldn't miss the shaking hand Carina pressed to her lips or the tear spilling from her eye. She reached toward him but stopped just short of making contact. Good thing. If she actually touched him, he might shatter.

"I remember hearing about the tragedy in the news." She withdrew her arm and wound her fingers together in her lap. "They never gave the name of the sole survivor fighting for his life in the hospital. That was you."

"That was me," he rasped. "I lost my taste for police work after that, and I'm still trying to figure out what I *do* have a taste for."

"Renovating your childhood home?"

Ryder shook his head. "I didn't grow up in that house. I was an adult when my folks moved there, shortly before the accident that took my dad. But I'm enjoying the reno project. I just don't see that sort of work as a long-term occupation. More like therapeutic busyness."

"You feel productive rather than merely stuck."

He darted a sharp look her way. "You get it."

She shrugged. "I'm well acquainted with seeking balm for grief. Fixing up a house seems like a healthy method. Some people do it in self-destructive ways. I was guilty of that after my husband died. I let someone take over my life, make all my decisions for me."

"Your aunt?"

Carina nodded.

"I get the impression she loves you," Ryder said, "but her way of showing it is to wrap you up so tightly in her care that you practically become an extension of herself. Not your own person anymore."

Her head swiveled his direction, eyes wide. "Now it's my turn to say you get it."

"I see why you're reluctant to seek her help with Jace."

"She'll interpret it as an admission that I can't cope independently."

"But it's not."

"No, it's not, but it's a necessity under the circumstances, and I'm completely confident in her ability to care for my son. That much is a relief. It'll be World War Three when I take him back and leave once more, and I'm going to feel guilty and miserable all over again that I'm hurting a person who loves me and wants to protect me. But that struggle is for later."

Ryder nodded. "We have more important things to think about right now."

"Where do we start uncovering the past?"

"The original crime scene—your childhood home right there in Tulsa."

Carina's face paled. "I don't even know the address. I've never been back there, you know. Not even anywhere near the neighborhood. I'm not sure how that's going to feel."

"Like a scab being ripped off a deep wound, I expect."

"Or like the curtain being peeled back from my memory of the murders and abduction."

Ryder pursed his lips. "Maybe, but don't count on it. I'm more interested in anything you can recall prior to the attack. What led up to it. You still have those memories, I assume."

"Sure, but I was seven years old. My parents wouldn't have let me in on anything going on in their lives that was potentially dangerous.

It's always been a fair assumption that what happened had to be connected to them."

Ryder frowned. "If there was something the killer wanted from your folks, it doesn't make sense to abduct you *after* doing away with them."

"It's a mystery. I'm sure the original investigators asked themselves that question, but I was too little to have any idea what they concluded."

"Hopefully, I'll be able to sneak a peek at those original files and find out. Meanwhile, what's the exact situation at your aunt's house? Anyone else living there?"

"Not since Jace and I left." Carina shook her head. "Aunt Althea's son, my cousin Frank, was twelve years old when I came to live with them, but he's been gone for years. Barely ever visits, much to my aunt's chagrin. He's got some sort of high-powered banking job in Oklahoma City."

Ryder sent her a sidelong look. Her tone said she didn't much care for Cousin Frank. "You don't sound sorry Frank isn't around."

She grimaced. "He was okay to me. Not warm and big-brotherly, but not hostile either. I guess we were never close is all."

"What about Frank's father? Not in the picture ever?"

"A bitter divorce before I was born, I'm told. Aunt Althea never talks about him, and I've certainly never seen him. I don't even know if he's still alive."

"Fair enough. We should—"

Carina's ringtone sounded before he could finish his suggestion that they call Detective Worthing with their whereabouts.

She fished her cell phone from her purse and shot him a stricken look. "*Unknown number* again."

Ryder raised his eyebrows. "The taunter calling so soon? Or maybe it's Worthing. We haven't let him know about our departure or asked him to contact us using my phone."

"Either way, we might as well get it over with." She swiped to answer and tapped again to activate the speaker. "Hello?" Her voice held a tentative quaver.

"Where are you?" Worthing's voice rolled across the airwaves like a peal of thunder.

"Why?" Ryder responded quickly to the urgency in the detective's tone.

Dead air extended across several heartbeats.

"You're not at home," the detective said. "I'm hearing road noises in the background."

Was that relief in the other man's voice?

"We're on our way to Tulsa to leave Carina's

little boy with her aunt for safekeeping while things get sorted out."

"Good thinking for multiple reasons."

"What do you mean?" Carina asked.

"Your rental house is on fire."

The air in Ryder's lungs turned to thin ice. Carina's head jerked around, toward her son in the back seat, a single thought written plainly in her eyes, which had turned to large *O*s. The same thought shivered through him.

What if they hadn't left when they did?

SIX

Carina's stomach roiled. "How bad is it?"

"How did the fire start?" Ryder's question overlapped hers.

"The answer to both of those questions is I don't know. I'm following the fire trucks to the scene. It'll help the firefighters to be assured you're not inside."

"Call us back then when you know more," Ryder said.

"Will do," Worthing answered, and the call ended.

Carina inhaled a shaky breath and let it out slowly. She looked at Ryder. "Are you thinking what I'm thinking?"

"Probably. First off, we can be thankful we weren't in the house when the fire started, and second, I'm not a fan of coincidence."

"Right. How likely is it that I'm the target of someone's vendetta, and the house where Jace and I are living randomly catches fire?"

Heat flared through her. "Is this vile person so intent on getting me that they'll endanger an innocent little boy? If I still had any reservations about leaving Jace in Aunt Althea's care, they've evaporated now. I need to call her and let her know we're coming. Should I tell her about the house fire?"

Ryder's shoulders rippled in a shrug. "If it comes up. Full disclosure is usually best. That way nothing comes back to bite you later. Maybe you can make the fire the main reason you're bringing Jace to her."

"She'll want to know details."

"We can't give her what we don't have."

Chest tight, Carina put the call through to her aunt. Two rings passed.

"Hello? Carina?" The woman sounded breathless, but she couldn't have needed to run to answer the call. She had to have been nearby. Probably in a marathon of baking— her aunt's equivalent of biting her fingernails.

"Aunt Althea, we're on our way to see you." Carina kept her tone casual and steady.

"You and Jace are coming? Praise God! You'll be safe here."

"Jace will be. I can't stay."

"Can't? Or won't?" Her aunt's voice went sharp.

"Both. There's no reason to think I'll be

safer at your place than anywhere else, but I need Jace to be safe while I stay on the move elsewhere."

"You're not going back to that little rental house in Argyle, are you?" The tone was disparaging.

"I can't. It's on fire."

"What?" The question was a shrill blast. "I knew moving away would bring you no good. I had a feeling—"

"Althea!" Carina put steel in her voice. "We were on our way to Tulsa before it started. An Argyle police detective called us about it. Will you look after Jace for me until the danger is past?"

"Of course I will, honey." Her aunt's voice went tender. "How could you doubt? But how is the danger going away for you? Are the police close to an arrest? Will they protect you?"

"Law enforcement personnel are doing everything they can to find out what's going on and stop whoever is behind it, but they don't have the people to offer me twenty-four-seven protection."

"So you're going into hiding?"

"Not exactly. I've got someone helping me figure out why someone is after me—a former police detective."

"You don't know any former police detectives. You're trusting a stranger? Or is he some sort of private detective you've hired?" Her aunt's tone became progressively more tense.

Carina opened her mouth but no words came out. How could she explain Ryder to a woman who made a professional career out of suspicion and paranoia? Not that the current situation didn't merit paranoia.

"Ma'am." Ryder spoke up, his deep voice steady and solid. "My name is Ryder Jameson. I was with the Oklahoma City Police Department for over a decade with an honorable record. The Argyle PD has confirmed that information to your niece. If it helps, in this situation you can think of me as sort of a cross between an unofficial private detective and a bodyguard."

"Aunt Althea," Carina said, "Ryder saved my life last night when the killer broke into my house." Did that explanation come out a bit breathy and rushed? Probably, but it was best to quickly overwhelm her aunt with information to forestall the third degree.

"Well then, sir, I thank you, I'm sure." Althea's tone came out prim, as if gratitude warred with residual suspicion—a normal condition for Carina's aunt.

"We'll be there in a few hours," Carina said. "We'll talk more then." She ended the call.

"I don't blame your aunt for having reservations about me," Ryder said. "The situation calls for extreme caution. But it would be helpful if you could give me a bit of background on her."

Carina rubbed the heels of her hands against her jeans-clad thighs. "Where do I start?"

"Basic background. Maybe whether she's your mother's sister or your father's sister."

"My mother's. No other siblings. About… hmm, six or seven years between them, I think. Althea was the elder. I remember my mother remarking to my dad once that Althea was the queen of big sisters." Carina let out a small laugh. "From my little princess-girl perspective, I figured being a queen had to be a good thing, but from an adult perspective and memory of the tone my mother used to make the statement, I've concluded Althea was as overbearing then as she can be now. In any case, the sisters weren't close. We rarely saw Aunt Althea or my cousin Frank while my parents were alive. Going to live with them felt like being plopped into a household with strangers."

"Okay." Ryder nodded. "What about your grandparents?"

"I never knew them. Some tragedy before I was born. At the age of seven, I wasn't much in the loop on details. Aunt Althea never spoke about her folks as I was growing up. *Her* orphaned condition seemed to take a big back seat to mine. I do know my mother's and aunt's maiden name, however. After Althea's divorce, she reclaimed the surname Kellmann, though I doubt my mother's name before she married my father has any bearing on current events. I have no idea what my aunt's married name was, and again, I don't see the significance."

"There probably isn't one," Ryder said. "But gathering these kinds of basics is part of any thorough investigation. Then the detective can begin to put together a coherent picture of the lives of those affected by the crime, and connections begin to be made that can have direct bearing on the solution to the case. If the reason your parents were murdered and you were kidnapped lies with your parents, then I need to know everything I can about them."

"Makes sense." Carina swiveled toward Ryder as far as her seat belt would allow. "My dad then. He was an only child. My paternal grandparents are still living, though I only ever met them in person once or twice before the tragedy and never afterward."

"Wow!" Ryder jerked back against his seat. "What's up with that?"

Carina laughed. "The story is unusual, but

not mysterious. They moved to Alaska to pastor a mission church in a deep rural area not served by overland roads. Their mission is only accessible by small plane or boat. No cell service or internet, but they love it. The off-grid life suits them. They communicate with the outside world via shortwave radio, but not with me since I've never had a short-wave radio. However, they never forget a birth-day or a special occasion for me or Jace, and they always send cards, letters or little gifts. You should see the adorable hand-stitched and beaded mukluks they sent for Jace's first birth-day—" She stopped abruptly with a gasp, tears stinging the backs of her eyes.

"What?" Ryder shot her a sharp glance.

"The mukluks are probably gone now."

"The fire? It's always the personal things that are the greatest loss. Photos, memorabilia. I'm so sorry."

Carina dabbed her fingers at the corners of her eyes. "I'm endlessly grateful we weren't at home when the fire started. Who knows what might have happened to us, but yes, there were a few precious and irreplaceable items in the house. Pictures, of course, but they're not tech-nically lost. Just the paper copies."

"Cloud account?"

She nodded, still swallowing emotion out of

her throat. Heaviness invaded her limbs and she slumped against the seat.

"You must be exhausted," Ryder said. "Interrupted sleep last night, nothing but stress today. Why don't you close your eyes and see if you can grab a snooze? I'll keep us headed toward Tulsa."

"You don't mind?" She swiveled her head toward him.

"Not at all."

Carina allowed her eyes to drift closed. She probably wouldn't be able to sleep, but a few minutes of peace and quiet would be wonderful. A long sigh feathered between her lips. Her hand found the control for the seat, and she lowered it backward into a comfortable tilt. Gentle darkness enveloped her.

And then the dream came.

Breath wheezing between clenched teeth, Carina curled herself tightly in the dark corner of her bedroom closet. The bad noises that had driven her from her bed were still happening downstairs. A strange man shouting. He sounded mean. Her father choking out answers. Her mother crying, begging. They sounded scared. The gallop of Carina's pulse in her ears drowned out the exact words.

A crash sounded, like glass shattering. Carina flinched and hugged her pajama-clad knees tightly to her thin chest. The voices rose in a jumble of anger and fear. A loud bang came. Then another one.

Silence crowded into her tiny closet. A fist squeezed Carina's lungs. Were Mommy and Daddy all right? Should she go and see? But her body was frozen in place.

A creak came from the staircase, followed by another. Every hair on Carina's body stood on end. Sounded like someone sneaking. Mom or Dad never crept around like that. Was the bad man coming? Was he looking for her? Would he find her?

A click signaled the latch on her door opening. Carina gasped in a breath of stuffy air. The hint of fabric softener smell from the clothes hanging above her tickled the back of her throat. She clapped both hands over her mouth to stifle a cough that would give her away.

The folding closet doors slid wide, mocking her attempt at silence. Carina gaped up at a dark shadow looming above her. The huge figure was outlined by the moonlight stealing in between the cracks of her window blinds, but the face remained in darkness.

The creature growled and reached for her.

* * *

Carina lunged upright, poker-stiff with the usual scream trapped in her windpipe.

"What's the matter?"

Ryder's taut question brought reality crashing back to her. They were on the road to Tulsa to take Jace to her aunt for safekeeping, and someone was out to kill her.

She inhaled deeply and let the air out slowly. "Just the old nightmare. How long was I asleep?"

"About an hour. This dream is about your childhood abduction?"

Carina grimaced. She preferred never to talk about hiding in the closet, the gunshots and the bad man coming for her, but she owed Ryder an explanation. In quick, terse sentences, she described the events in the dream.

"You remember this?" Ryder asked.

She shook her head. "I don't know if the nightmare is accurate memory or if it's a hodgepodge of emotion rather than actual experience."

"Sounds real to me," Ryder said. "And terrifying for anyone, much less a young child."

Carina nodded acknowledgment of the kind sympathy in his tone. The chill of the nightmare was receding and her breathing was evening out. Fussy noises started coming from the back seat. Carina looked over her shoulder to find Jace kicking and scowling in a way that she knew would soon turn to all-out wailing.

"We'd better take the next opportunity for a break. He needs to be fed and changed."

"A snack and coffee at the tables inside sounds great to me, too. Plus, we should gas up."

A few minutes later, they pulled into a sprawling truck stop, complete with a large convenience store and combination pizzeria and sub shop. Carina gathered her son and his paraphernalia together. While she did that, Ryder unbuckled his shoulder holster and tucked it and the larger of his two guns into the glove compartment of the SUV. She raised her eyebrows at him, and he sent her a quick smile.

"I'm still wearing a pistol at my waist, but it's covered by my shirt," he said. "I don't want to freak people out in the store with my shoulder piece."

"Good thinking." She nodded and left Ryder pumping gas.

Carina headed through the heat of a cloudless summer afternoon toward the coolness of the ladies' bathrooms inside the convenience store. Within thirty minutes, Jace had been fed, and she and Ryder had enjoyed a snack at one of the small tables near the eateries. They turned toward the SUV, Ryder carrying a contented and smiling Jace.

A pang shot through Carina. To anyone watching them, they must look like a normal, happy family unit. Not a soul would be able to guess the true situation. Amazing how deceptive appearances could be. She increased her pace.

Suddenly, Carina halted on a gasp.

Ryder stopped beside her. "What?" His brows drew together.

She dredged up a smile. "Nothing earth-shaking. I forgot Jace's stuffed bunny at the table where we had our snacks. Get him buckled in, okay? I'll be right back." She did an about-face and trotted off for the building.

"Wait, Carina!"

Ryder's urgent tone barely carried over a sudden shriek of rubber against pavement. Carina whirled toward the noise. A cherry-red sports car with tinted windows barreled straight for her, engine roaring. The shiny grill grinned like a maniacal beast.

Clutching Jace to his side with one arm, Ryder swept his gun from its pancake holster with the other. No time to fine-tune his aim, especially when firing one-handed. He had only the small hope that any shot would make the driver flinch away from his target.

The pistol bucked against Ryder's palm. A sharp report echoed in his ears, along with the plink of a bullet striking metal as it punctured some part of the vehicle. The tail of the sports car fish-tailed as the driver swerved reflexively from the gun threat. Then the lethal red rocket swept past, engine gunning out of the lot with the harsh odor of burning rubber.

"Carina!" Ryder called.

Her figure lay facedown and still on the pavement several yards from him. Vaguely, he registered that Jace was clutching his neck, wailing. Cradling the little guy close, Ryder hurried to Carina. The breath labored in his tight chest as he knelt by her side.

Had she been clipped by the vehicle? She hadn't been struck full-on, he'd noted that much. She was breathing and didn't appear to be bleeding. Her limbs were aligned, so no evident breaks in the bones.

Ryder lifted his head and gazed around at scattered onlookers who were staring open-mouthed and frozen in place. "Someone—anyone—call for the police and an ambulance!"

The lash of his tongue seemed to break people from their shocked paralysis, and they began pecking at their cell screens. Were any of them actually placing the 9-1-1 call? Most seemed to be taking pictures or videos of the scene. Ryder ground his teeth together.

One of the checkout staff stepped outside. "Cops and EMTs on the way," she announced with a wide-eyed nod at Ryder.

"Thank you."

A groan from Carina snapped his attention back to her. She lifted her head.

"Stay still," he said.

"Jace?" Her voice was faint, tremulous.

"I've got him. He's safe."

She puffed out a breath and, with a soft groan, began to raise herself.

"Be still," he said again. "Help is on the way."

"It's okay." She managed to roll over and sit up. "I'm not hurt. Not much anyway. I made a leaping dive, and the car missed me. But I felt the wind of its passing."

Ryder followed her glance toward her left knee. A ragged tear in her jeans revealed a nasty abrasion beginning to weep pinpricks of blood. Carina turned her hands up and displayed a matched set of skinned palms.

"Reminds me of the time I was ten and fell off my bike on the way home from a friend's house." A high-pitched giggle spurted between her lips.

Equal parts shock and hysteria, no doubt. Ryder couldn't blame her for either reaction. She'd nearly been mowed down by tons of accelerating vehicle. Nothing about the incident could have been accidental. Yet, as deadly as the attack had been, it smacked of opportunistic amateur hour, a complete contrast with the professional hit attempted on Carina's first night in Argyle. Did this indicate the hitter's client was now taking matters into his or her own hands, or did Carina have two different parties after her? One patient and cautious— and with pockets deep enough to pay for what he wanted done—and the other impatient and reckless and desperate enough to attempt murder on his own? Either possibility was chilling.

In the distance, but approaching fast, sirens wailed. Ryder turned his head toward the sound, but at the soft grip of a hand on his arm, he returned his attention to Carina.

"I'm going to get up now. I can't stand one more second of sitting in the middle of the tarmac being the subject of onlookers' Snapchats."

"I'm sure the EMTs would recommend you stay put."

"Nevertheless."

Ryder bowed to the determination in her

steely gaze. "Would sitting in the car work for you?"

She nodded. "When I'm situated, you can give Jace to me."

The little boy had stopped crying, but he still whimpered.

"You got it." Ryder lent the support of his arm as Carina drew herself to her feet.

A cheer and a smattering of applause met the action. Carina offered a half smile, half grimace as Ryder guided her toward the passenger seat of her vehicle. Her step was surprisingly firm. Apparently, she'd been telling the truth that she was not badly hurt, but he'd let the EMTs make their educated assessment.

They approached now. A squad car whipped into the lot followed by an ambulance. The cacophony set Jace wailing again. Ryder handed the child to his mother, and the tot buried his face in Carina's shoulder. She patted his back and crooned comforting words to him.

The next half hour was consumed with medical examinations and statements to police officers. One officer checked and cleared Ryder's license to carry a firearm while the other called in an all-points bulletin on the attack car. Ryder had captured the license plate number, but a quick consultation of the police database said the sports car had been reported stolen this morning. Of course it had. And it didn't take much imagination to surmise it would be found abandoned somewhere in the not too distant future.

Ryder told Carina his assumption, and she agreed. Stealing a car and then abandoning it echoed what the person in the gorilla mask had done. If this were an MO, then it could well be that the masked driver from this morning was the same person as the attempted hit-and-run driver. Because of the darkly tinted windows in the sports car, none of the witnesses—including Ryder and Carina—had been able to make out a face behind the wheel.

The EMTs determined that Carina was indeed only bruised and abraded. No bones were broken, nothing dislocated, and she had not hit her head when she fell, so concussion was not a consideration. The emergency medical team cleaned and bandaged the wounds and recommended she come to the hospital for a further checkup, but she declined decisively.

"We need to get where we're going as quickly as we can," she told Ryder with enormous, pleading eyes. "Before this attacker finds another vehicle and comes after us again, Jace needs to be placed somewhere safe, and I need to get myself far away from him."

"Agreed," Ryder said, and tension visibly melted from Carina's shoulders.

She must have assumed he would try to insist on a further medical exam. In most circumstances, he would have done so, but Jace's safety had to be the priority so they could be free to carry on the investigation that would reunite mother and son free from fear of attack. Provided they succeeded in solving this mystery and seeing the perpetrator or perpetrators behind bars where they belonged.

Ryder firmed his jaw as he climbed in behind the steering wheel of Carina's SUV. They *would* figure out what was going on, and they *would* see justice done. Failure was not an option.

One of the attending officers knocked on Ryder's window, and he lowered it.

"You're cleared to leave, sir, ma'am." He nodded across at Carina. "We've got your contact information and will update you when we know anything."

Carina leaned forward and peered past Ryder at the young officer. "Thank you for everything…ah, Blake." Her gaze lifted from his name badge to the guy's face, and she shot him a smile.

What it had cost her to respond with calm cheer in this gut-twisting situation, Ryder could only imagine. But the smile seemed to knock the guy for a loop. His face grew pink, and his expression went slack. Clearly, he wasn't the only one to think Carina was a stunner. Ryder powered the window upward, forcing the guy to step back. What was up with this territorial instinct? He was with Carina in a professional capacity—albeit an unofficial one—and it was best he stayed mindful of that fact.

They got on the road again, neither of them speaking. Jace, too, was quiet in the back. Perhaps the excitement had exhausted him and he'd gone to sleep. Carina shifted in her seat then a short time later shifted again.

"Are you in pain?" he asked.

"Minor discomfort physically. Completely overwhelmed mentally and emotionally."

"Perfectly understandable."

Mouth set in a grim line, she glanced over at him. "Thank you for saving my life once again. Sure, I made a flying leap, but if that car hadn't swerved, it would still have hit me."

"My pleasure. I just wish we could have caught the driver."

"You and me both." She huffed. "You'd think Detective Worthing would be calling any time to update us on my house fire."

"Why don't you go ahead and give him a call? Put it on speaker."

Carina got on the phone and Worthing answered on the second ring.

"I was just about to get back to you," he said. "Definitely arson. An incendiary device was mounted on the electrical box attached to the house. Fairly sophisticated workmanship."

"A bomb?" Carina's voice squeaked.

Ryder's mouth went dry. "Any collateral damage?"

"No one got hurt. It wasn't really a bomb. More like an aggressive fire starter. No other property was damaged. In fact, the damage wasn't all that extensive except for a hole in the kitchen wall and quite a lot of smoke from what turned out to be a relatively contained blaze. The fire department had it out fairly quickly."

"Not a total loss then," Carina said with a marginally lighter note in her voice.

Silence for a couple of heartbeats. "No-o-o," Worthing drawled, "not a total loss of the home's contents, but the place isn't going to be inhabitable any time soon what with all the smoke and water damage. You should be able to salvage some personal belongings, particularly anything that was on the second floor."

"That's a snippet of good news then, Detective Worthing."

"I have another snippet of that for you," the detective said. "One of the officers injured when the contract killer escaped has been released from the hospital, and the other one is out of danger and on the road to recovery."

"That *is* good news." Carina's tone was emphatic, and a smile flashed briefly on her face.

"We've had another incident on our end," Ryder said, and filled the detective in on the hit-and-run attempt. "If you want to be in the loop, I'll have Carina text you the contact details for the officers who took the call. They left us their card."

"Do that, and I'll be in touch with them. You folks take care now, and that's not idle small talk."

"Agreed," Carina said and tapped the screen to end the call. She let out a snort. "What could possibly happen next? The situation would be unbelievable if it weren't real."

"Hang in there, Carina. We're about to turn this thing around and go on the offensive."

She sent him a bleak look and turned away to look out the side window. Frowning, Ryder concentrated on his driving. Mildly undulating Oklahoma terrain, interrupted now and then with billboards, flowed past on either side of the road. Cattle pastures alternated with harvested hay fields dotted with round bales. Rural Americana, so peaceful in appearance.

Carina's head abruptly swiveled toward him. "How did the creep know where we were? Did you see that flashy red sports car following us from Argyle?"

Ryder's stomach bottomed out and he mentally kicked himself. Why hadn't he already asked himself those questions?

"No, I did not see the car following us," he said. "And I certainly would have noticed a vehicle like that. It had to have arrived in the lot while we were inside the convenience store."

"Oh, no!"

"What?" Ryder's breath caught and he darted her a piercing look.

"I never did go in and get Jace's stuffed bunny."

"Oh." The simple syllable must have conveyed the wealth of his puzzlement because it drew a brief chuckle from her.

"You have no idea how tragic it would be if Mr. Cottontail were the only stuffy Jace would sleep with."

"Lots of howling and fussing and no rest for the weary?" Ryder offered her a lopsided smile.

"Beyond imagination. Happily, I still have Ms. Kitty. Jace likes her almost as much."

"Whew!" Ryder made an exaggerated point of wiping pretend sweat off his brow.

His reward was a burst of genuinely light-hearted laughter from his front-seat passenger. A resentful mewl came from Jace, and Carina clapped a hand over her mouth.

"He's sleeping," she whispered. "No stuffy necessary for that to happen in his car seat. I don't want to wake him up."

"Back to your earlier question about how this creep found us at the gas station," Ryder said. "We need to figure that out. And I want to know why it was necessary to burn your house even though, if he was following us by some amazing invisible means, he must have known we weren't in it. Is he desperate to keep you from returning to Argyle?"

"So many questions, so few answers."

Ryder opened his mouth then the words stalled on his tongue. Did he really want to ask her this? She was spooked enough. Then again, holding back on any possibility could endanger her further.

He cleared his throat. "It almost seems like two separate kinds of perpetrators are conducting this vendetta against you."

"Two?"

"One of them is high-tech and high-budget. The other seizes opportunity and operates in ruthless but reckless meanness."

Minutes ticked past as Carina sat in pale-faced silence.

At last, she pivoted toward him. "I'm not saying there couldn't be multiple parties involved, but I can't buy into two separate vendettas for two separate reasons. There's got to be a unifying factor we're not seeing."

"Yet," Ryder added, and she nodded.

He'd been thinking while she'd been sitting, quietly ruminating on his suggestion. That red car had not been following them based on keeping them in sight, but there was another possibility—one that was perhaps even scarier. A wayside rest stop was coming up. Ryder slowed the car and signaled for the turn.

"Why are we stopping again?" Carina's tone was sharp.

"There's something I need to check out before we go another mile."

"Okay?"

He brought the car to a halt in the parking lot some distance from any other vehicle. There were several in the lot, including a couple of RVs and one semi parked in the special lot for big trucks.

"Sit tight," he told Carina as he got out.

His eyes scanned the area. A group of people loitered near the bathrooms—a man, a woman and three kids of varying ages. Clearly a family unit. Several lone individuals and a few couples occupied benches or picnic tables under shade trees. Several people were walking along the sidewalks. There was nothing suspicious in anyone's movements, and no one was paying attention to Ryder or to Carina's vehicle.

Reasonably satisfied that no hostiles were in the area, Ryder proceeded to run his fingers under the bumpers and around the wheel wells. Under the rear passenger wheel well, he found what he'd thought he might. The small object resisted at first, but a jerk of Ryder's fingers overcame the magnetic attraction that had affixed it to the metal on the car. For long seconds, he stared at the miniature rectangular box in his hand. Then he stood and carried the thing to Carina's window. She powered it down and stared at him with raised eyebrows.

He showed her the small object. "This is how we were followed without anyone having to be in sight of us."

"A tracker?" Her eyes went wide.

"Technology again. Planning."

"And yet trying to run me down at a gas station was opportunistic."

"Impulsive. Yes. I wouldn't be surprised if the person who thought to plant the tracker isn't upset with the sports car driver for spoiling whatever more well-considered setup was in the works by the brains of their partnership, conspiracy or whatever you might want to call their relationship."

"That would be a good thing, right? Confusion in the ranks?"

Ryder nodded and attempted a smile. "Hopefully." Or maybe the conflict would boil over into redoubled attempts to get the job done.

SEVEN

Carina stared at the small black box. Her insides clenched. Someone with evil intent had been tracking them—was still tracking them. Another attack could happen at any moment.

"When would anyone have found opportunity to put a tracker on my car?" she asked. "I assume it would need to have been after the failed attempt to shoot me in my bed."

"Yes, after that, but not while we were parked in the police lot. It must have been while we were in the store buying the security system. By then, they would already have had the device planted on your house to start the fire. If that didn't take care of us, they would have wanted to know where we went."

"Makes frightening sense." Carina shuddered. "Destroy that thing, and let's get out of here."

A tight grin split Ryder's face. "I've got a better idea. I'll be right back."

Carina craned her neck as her gaze followed Ryder's trotting figure to the back lot occupied by the RVs and a long-haul semi. He stopped near the passenger's-side front wheel of the semi's cab. Seconds later, he ran back to their SUV.

"You put the tracker on the semi?" she asked as Ryder slid into the driver's seat.

"Let the bad guys follow it to Timbuktu or wherever the truck is going. Whenever they decide to close in, and they come in sight of it, they'll know right away we found the tracker, moved it and sent them on a wild-goose chase."

"But by then we will have had time to drop Jace off and be somewhere else."

"You got it."

Carina smiled as Ryder headed their vehicle toward the highway. Something like a clenched fist released its grip around her heart and she leaned her head back against the seat rest. They stood a possibility now of getting Jace to safety and finding a little bit of that for themselves somewhere else—while incognito—in Tulsa.

An hour later, they entered the outskirts of the city, and Carina gave Ryder directions to her aunt's place in Tulsa's southwestern suburb of Oakhurst. Soon, they were cruising up a quiet residential street toward the house that had been Carina's home for the majority of her youth. For some reason—probably consecutive near-death experiences—she viewed the house with new eyes now.

It was a bungalow-style dwelling perched on a small green lawn in a solidly middle-class neighborhood. The home was mostly single-story, but with a partial second story built into the sloping roof. Dormer windows indicated the location of the second-story room. At first, that upper room had been Cousin Frank's space—an area that had been off-limits to her as long as Frank was part of the household. Later, the second story had become her room when Frank went off to college in Oklahoma City and never moved back home. So, really, there was no nook or cranny of this house that was not familiar to her. Yet today, vividly outlined by the setting sun, the structure seemed alien, a place she'd never been before and maybe didn't want to go.

Carina shook herself as Ryder slid the vehicle to the curb outside the bungalow. What was the matter with her? Since the loss of her parents, this house had been a haven for her. And now it would be so for Jace in their time of need.

Firming her jaw, Carina got out of the SUV and opened the rear door to collect her little boy. He'd awakened a short time ago and was now fussing to be held or changed or fed—or all of the above.

"Hush, baby boy," she said to him as she gathered his warm weight into her arms.

Jace immediately quieted and snuggled into her shoulder.

Ryder had come around the vehicle and was reaching in for the diaper bag when a shrill feminine voice let out a wordless cry.

Carina turned to find her aunt hurrying toward them, thin arms stretched out. Althea had always been slender and narrow, but as happened with certain body types, age had rendered her nearly gaunt. Her loose-fitting blouse and slacks did little to soften her angularity, and the short-cropped gray hair emphasized the sharpness of her features. Her expression, however, was warm and welcoming.

"Oh, my darling," she said, beaming at Carina. "I'm so glad you came home…and brought my sweet little Jacey-bear with you." She snatched Jace and hugged him close. "Come on in. Your rooms are ready and waiting like always."

"We're not here to stay, Aunt Althea," Carina said.

If only her tone hadn't come out with an

edge. But they were in a terrifying situation, and her aunt was acting as if they'd come for an extended, perhaps even permanent, stay. Apparently, Althea's hope sprang eternal.

Her aunt sniffed, spared Carina a brow-arched glance, then turned her attention to Ryder.

He stepped forward and held out his hand. "Ryder Jameson. We spoke on the phone."

Althea shook Ryder's hand but narrowed her pale green eyes. "You've been helping my girl and her little boy."

"That's right."

"Good." Althea jerked a nod. "Let's get inside then."

The woman turned on her heel and marched toward her front door, bearing Jace like a prize, with the remaining adults trailing in her wake as if she were leading a triumphal procession. Carina shot Ryder a glance and shrugged. He returned a small smile and a wink.

Something tilted inside Carina. The man was too attractive, too capable, too courageous and faithful for her peace of mind. They were together right now in a situation that was anything but romantic. What was the matter with her that she wished they were dropping off Jace so they could go on a date?

Get real, girl! Ryder was no longer a cop because he was struggling to come to terms with his own survival when the rest of his team had died violently. Didn't that mean protecting her and Jace was a penance project, nothing personal at all? She would need to be okay with that because, if not for him, she would already be in the morgue.

Carina firmed her wayward heart as they stepped through the front door. Immediately, they came into a shotgun-style living room with a hallway visible through a door to the right. As she well knew, the hallway led to two bedrooms, a small office that had been converted into Jace's nursery, and a bathroom. Ahead, a wooden half wall partially hid a small dining room, and beyond it was a compact but fully equipped kitchen. Neither the spare décor nor the bland color palette had changed in all the years Carina had lived there. The familiar scents of cooking and baking— her aunt's favorite hobbies—wrestled with the equally familiar but sharper odor of furniture polish. Housecleaning was Althea's next most frequent occupation. More as a duty than a delight, however. Far be it from her that her ladies' Bible study group should spy a speck of dust.

"I've got a lasagna in the oven," her aunt said, "and I've baked your favorite chocolate-chunk cookies." Althea led the way into the dining room and indicated they should take seats.

Jace's spare high chair that Carina had left behind when she'd moved was set up on one side of the table, exactly where his chair was always positioned. Carina swallowed a sigh. Back to square one. At least her aunt was pretending it was so.

"I need to change Jace," she told Althea, "but I'm sure we'll be glad of some food when I get back."

"Thank you for your trouble." Ryder nodded at the older woman and settled into a chair at the table.

Carina took Jace and bore him to the nursery. The crib and the changing table were gone because she had taken them to Argyle with her, but the narrow daybed that had been in this room for as long as Carina could remember made an okay spot to lay her son down while she changed his diaper. In a few months, she'd start thinking about potty training him and leaving the diapers behind, but not yet.

Her memory suddenly conjured the image of the hit man and his gun, standing in her bedroom. She shivered.

Back in the dining room, she found Ryder and her aunt chatting as Althea bustled back and forth from kitchen to dining room, setting the table. The fresh coffee smell identified the beverage steaming in the mug sitting before Ryder. Carina deposited Jace in the high chair, where her son immediately grabbed the sippy cup on the tray and began to guzzle the milk inside it. Carina proceeded into the kitchen to pour herself a glass of water. Coffee would only render her more jittery than she already was.

"Has Ryder explained the situation to you?" she asked her aunt as the woman pulled a richly fragrant pan of lasagna, cheese bubbling, from the oven and set it on top of the stove.

Althea stood straight and frowned. "I can't understand why this is happening. Maybe it *wouldn't* have happened if you'd stayed here where you belong."

"Maybe it would, ma'am, and you'd be hurt because you were in the way." Ryder's deep, no-nonsense voice drew a gasp from Carina's aunt.

The woman turned to him and stared, unblinking. "Do you really think so?"

"I think it's a possibility. The best way you can help is to keep Little Bit while we try to figure this out. Can you do that?"

"Of course." Althea lifted her pointed chin.

"My pleasure. You'll keep in touch, won't you?" The woman's tone was as needy and uncertain as Carina had ever heard it.

"Of course we will." Carina grasped her aunt's bony hand with her own.

"Good." Ryder nodded. "But you won't pry me out of here until I've had some of that delicious-smelling lasagna."

Aunt Althea beamed at him, and Carina suppressed a smile. Ryder had hit her aunt's sweet spot when it came to winning her approval. She lived to feed people. Carina's heart twinged. It must genuinely be difficult for Althea when she was home alone with no one to fuss over. Too bad her son seemed always to do his level best to keep his distance from his mother, but in a way Carina could understand. Aunt Althea's neediness drove people away from her, the opposite of the effect the woman desired.

"Frank is coming for a visit in a couple of days," Althea announced in jubilant tones, almost as if she had picked up on Carina's thoughts. "I hope this mess will be over so all of us can have a nice visit. It's been too long since everyone was together in this house."

Unsettled, Carina mouthed a noncommittal response and helped dish up the food. Frank often promised to visit, but rarely followed through. If Frank let his mother down again, Althea's disappointment would render her even more difficult to deal with.

After supper, Ryder brought Jace's car seat inside for Althea's use, and he also retrieved the play yard they had brought along so the toddler would have a safe place to sleep. He set the latter up in Jace's old room. Carina used the time to cuddle her little boy and get him interested in a few toys Althea had retained when they'd left. Somehow, a couple of hours slipped away and Jace was rubbing his eyes against the sleep that wanted to claim him.

"I'll put him down for the night," she told her aunt. "Then Ryder and I can leave without him realizing we're going."

More minutes passed and by the time Carina had given her aunt a last hug and was following Ryder to the door for leave-taking, full darkness had fallen. At the threshold, he switched off the outside light that illuminated the stoop, gestured for her to remain inside and stepped through the door. The light from the living room outlined his alert stance, his head swiveling from left to right and back again.

At last, he turned toward her. "Normal night insect noises and nothing appears out of place, but that's no guarantee. Let's hustle."

He took her free hand—the other one held

a sack of her aunt's cookies—and drew her down the steps and up the sidewalk to the SUV. At their trespass into the warm darkness, the nearby insects went silent. Ryder held Carina's door as she climbed in then shut it after her with hardly a glance in her direction, his gaze continuing to sweep their environment.

"Where are we going?" she asked him as he settled in behind the wheel and pulled away from the curb.

"Lots of decent, moderately priced hotels around. We can get a couple of rooms without it setting us back too much."

"Okay," she said with a glance over her shoulder at her aunt's house fading behind them. Was she doing the right thing leaving her son there? But what else could she do?

Carina turned to Ryder. "Do you think these people after me know about my aunt?"

"I'd be surprised if they didn't know a lot about you. Lowlifes don't send hit men after random targets, but Jace is still better off away from us."

"Away from me, you mean."

"Us. You're not alone, Carina." He glanced at her, but the darkness hid his expression.

Warmth loosened the knot in her stomach. She wasn't alone, and her companion seemed handpicked for this situation. Had to be a God thing.

Thank You, Lord, for looking after me and Jace. Thank You for Ryder. Please help us figure things out quickly. And, God—Carina stole a look at her companion's shadowed profile—*please help me not to fall into dependence but to walk away gracefully when this is over and he wants to get on with his life.*

By the time they arrived at a reasonably priced franchise hotel, Ryder was almost certain they had not been followed and were not under surveillance. Also, there was no reason to believe their pursuers would have the kinds of resources that would allow them to flag their use of his credit card to rent the rooms. That capacity belonged to serious black hat hackers or government agencies with judicial permission to trace specific individuals. He and Carina should be safe enough overnight, and a good night's sleep could only help their clarity of mind tomorrow. Within minutes, they had received their room keys—adjoining, at his request—then gotten back into the SUV.

Ryder pulled the vehicle around to the back of the hotel so it wouldn't be visible from the highway running past the building. As he shut the engine off, he gazed at the woman beside him. Pole lights in the parking lot provided enough illumination for him to make out the expression on her face. Exhaustion, for sure, as evidenced by the dark smudges under her eyes. Her lips were drawn into a thin line and her brows had pulled together, creating a slight V in the skin between them.

"We're going to get some rest now," he told her. "Tomorrow I'll call in a few favors and see if we can access the cold case investigation files."

Carina nodded. "At least we have a next step in mind." She met his gaze. The corners of her mouth attempted to curve upward, failed, and curved downward instead.

"Hang in there. We're *going* to figure this out."

"Are we?" The hands in her lap clenched into fists. "I feel like my life has exploded, and I don't have the faintest idea how to put the pieces back together again."

"A day at a time, putting one foot in front of the other."

She snorted and managed a faint smile this time. "And stop being so pitiful, right?"

Ryder cupped his hand over one of her fists. "You're anything but pitiful."

"Thank you." She opened her fist and squeezed the hand he'd offered.

Warmth curled around his heart. Her hand felt good in his, right somehow. He gave himself a mental shake. He shouldn't—couldn't—think that way. Gently, he released her.

Carina turned and reached for the door latch.

"Let me get out first," he said quickly. "I'll grab our bags then let you out, and we'll walk in quickly together."

She sent him a questioning look.

"I don't think there's any threat nearby," he said, "but we're going to be cautious all the same."

"I can do cautious." The smile flickered again.

They followed the plan and hustled together through the warm night. His keycard got them through the rear entrance into the building. The air-conditioning welcomed them, along with the faint odors of hotel carpeting and this morning's complimentary breakfast that had been served in the small dining room up the hallway. They took a set of painted concrete stairs up to the second floor and soon were standing in front of their respective rooms, ready to let themselves inside.

"Don't answer your door unless you know it's me," Ryder told her as he readied to wave his keycard over the sensor.

"And here I had my heart set on room service." She let out a tense chuckle.

"Barely funny." He shook his head and offered a slight grin.

Her shoulders visibly relaxed and she returned the grin. "Thank you again…for everything. Good night." She swiped her keycard and let herself into her room.

Ryder did the same. The room was compact but clean and had everything necessary for a comfortable short-term stay. The queen-sized bed beckoned his weary body, but he had a few things to take care of first, like cleaning and reloading the gun he'd had to fire this afternoon. He could only hope he wouldn't have to use it again, but these people after Carina were deadly serious—literally. He needed to be ready to match their intensity.

Half an hour later, Ryder finally crawled under the covers and switched off the wall lamp over the bed. His gun sat ready next to him on the bedside table. A faint patina of city lights infiltrated the room through chinks in the window blinds, and a soft glow from the hallway lights crept in under the doorway, but the darkness was more than adequate for restful sleep. Managing to keep his eyes closed was the problem. The events from the last twenty-four hours kept playing through his mind, and his cop brain tugged at each item, attempting to tease meaning from the details that might lead to an understanding of why Carina was a target and who was behind the attempts on her life.

No sounds passed through the wall from the room next door. Maybe she was managing to get some much needed sleep. The hallway was silent, as well. No foot traffic at all. Gradually, Ryder faded into slumber.

Something brought Ryder swimming back to consciousness. He stiffened. Where was he? Oh, yes, the hotel. He lifted his head from the pillow and glanced at the digital readout from the bedside clock. Four a.m. Then he lay still, listening.

There had been a sound, hadn't there?

Nothing reached him from the neighboring room where Carina was hopefully enjoying peaceful slumber. No obvious noises of people passing by in the hallway. Except…there it came again. Not the boisterous sounds of a group of partiers returning to their hotel. Or even the businesslike tread of someone heading for a room. It was something far more insidious. The whisper of stealthy feet on the hall carpeting. Then a few murmured words in a masculine timbre, barely audible.

Ryder slid from the bed, yanked on his jeans and T-shirt, then grabbed his pistol. On swift bare feet, he reached his door and silently slid the chain from its mooring. Unlatching the dead bolt was going to make a noise. He needed his timing to be seamless as he turned it, opened the door and lunged out into the hallway, gun at the ready, hoping not to terrify an unsuspecting hotel patron returning to their room. But he couldn't risk assuming the sounds he'd heard were innocent when they had been so suspiciously sneaky.

A muted click carried to his ears, shooting a river of ice down his spine. Someone in the hallway near at hand had undone a dead bolt. A certain type of magnet could perform that action from the outside.

Ryder twisted his own bolt, yanked open his door and leaped into brightness. He squinted even as he aimed in two-handed shooter's crouch at a pair of large men in dark suits, ski masks covering their faces. The men stood in front of Carina's door, which hung open to the length of its chain. One man, his back to Ryder, was lifting a pair of bolt cutters toward the obstruction while the other turned at the sudden movement, the gun in his hand spitting fire.

The bullet nearly parted the hair over Ryder's left ear, its deadly whine like a giant bee. He squeezed the trigger on his own weapon, the sharp explosion and the buck against his palms familiar—as if it hadn't been months since he'd visited a shooting range. The gunman yelped and dropped his weapon. The one with the cutters whirled and threw the bulky tool at him. Ryder dodged the flying implement as the pair took to their heels. He raised his gun again, but they'd darted around the corner toward the stairway.

Ryder raced forward in pursuit even as muted screams reached him from surrounding rooms. Was one of the screams Carina's? He couldn't stop to reassure her. If he could capture even one of the suspects, maybe they would get answers about what was going on.

At the corner where the pair had disappeared, Ryder halted and peered into the adjacent hallway. No sign of the fleeing men, but a dollop of blood on the carpet said he'd at least winged one of the assailants. Ahead, the metal stairway door was slowly easing closed. He trotted to the door, gun at the ready, and halted its full closure with his bare foot. The stampede of shoes against concrete echoed in the stairwell. Every other step displayed another dollop of blood. The guy wasn't bleeding out, but he was hurting.

Pulse surging in his veins, Ryder headed onto the stairs, avoiding the blood trail with his bare feet. His swift passage made hardly any sound at all. Behind and above him, the stairwell door groaned open, and the hairs on the back of his neck prickled.

"Ryder!" Carina's voice called, sharp and shrill.

"Stay back," he hissed urgently.

No time to stop now. He reached the ground-floor hallway to find the hotel's rear exit closing in similar fashion to the stairway door. Ryder slowed and crept to the exit. Barreling through that portal, outlined in the light from the hotel hallway, would not be wise. The bolt-cutter guy might also have a gun and could shoot him from the cover of darkness.

Standing to the side of the door, he peered out through the glass. There! Two bulky shadows flitted quickly through the parking lot. The thugs weren't waiting in ambush, but merely trying to get away. Ryder stepped forward and reached for the door handle.

"Police! Halt where you are and drop your weapon!"

The masculine bellow came from behind him, farther up the hallway leading to the front desk. The glass in the door in front of Ryder reflected a beefy uniformed officer in shooter's stance, gun extended. Scalp prickling, Ryder obediently froze. He released his grip on his pistol and it thudded to the carpet. Then he slowly raised his arms.

Outside, the screech of tires against asphalt told him the assailants had made good their escape. As if that wasn't bad enough, now he was looking at time in a police interrogation room until the incident got sorted out.

To his left, Carina arrived at the bottom of the stairs, pajama-clad, disheveled and breathless. She gazed at him then at the cop behind him and went white.

Ryder groaned. If he got hauled in for questioning, Carina might be left alone and vulnerable.

EIGHT

"How did those thugs find us?" Carina asked Ryder, who was sitting across from her at a large table in a conference room at the police station. "We got rid of the tracker."

A pair of wary uniformed officers who'd happened to be doing their nightly drive-by of the hotel when the shots were fired had escorted them immediately out of the hotel. Carina was still clad in her pajamas.

Then she and Ryder had spent a couple of hours in separate, sterile interrogation rooms answering dozens of questions. Once their story was borne out by the physical evidence of the thugs' dropped gun and bolt cutters, and backed up by an examination of the second-floor hallway video recording, Carina and Ryder had been reunited and situated in more congenial surroundings. The detective in charge of their case had gone to telephone Detective Worthing in Argyle to discuss the larger situation concerning whoever was after Carina.

Mugs of steaming coffee sat in front of each of them. She lifted her cup, sipped at the bitter beverage and grimaced. Too bad a little caffeine wasn't likely to banish the weariness that mantled her slumped shoulders.

Ryder set his coffee mug on the table with a soft *thunk*. Carina winced. He must be beyond frustrated, as she was, that the suspects had gotten away.

"I expect whoever is behind these attacks figured out we must be headed for Tulsa," he said. "That's the direction we were going, and you have roots here. The misdirection with the tracker was only ever a hopeful ploy. Once the assumption of our destination was made, they were also likely to assume you wouldn't risk staying with anyone you knew and cared about. Whoever this is must have influence and contacts. I imagine they located us the old-fashioned way—by putting the word out to watch for a couple with our names or meeting our descriptions checking into a hotel. Who knows? The guy at the front desk might have turned us in."

"We were that easy to find?" Carina grimaced.

Ryder frowned. "We already know the person behind the attempted hit on you must have deep pockets, and they were clever with that tracker business, but I didn't foresee access to a network of human resources. I'm sorry."

Ryder's lips were set in a grim line and heightened color tinted his cheeks. His stare was fixed on his coffee mug as if the dark liquid within provided a fascinating study. Carina reached out and covered one of his hands with her own. His eyes lifted to meet hers. Did she read surprise there?

"I don't blame you for anything," she said. "You saved my life. Again. We're adjusting our understanding of the situation as things happen."

He scowled. "I don't like to keep playing catch-up. It's about time we got a lead that will help us nail these perps."

The door opened, drawing their attention. Detective Graham, who had taken charge of their case, entered the room bearing a medium-sized file box. He set the box on the table and surveyed them soberly.

"Detective Worthing verified everything you told us about what went on in Argyle," he said. "He's plenty worried about you two."

"We're not exactly easy in our minds either." Ryder's tone was extra dry.

"Worthing said you think this vendetta

against Carina has something to do with her parents' murders and her kidnapping when she was a child. Of course, it's not exactly protocol to share police files with civilians or even ex-cops." Graham twiddled his fingers noisily against the box lid.

Carina's stomach did a little jump, and across from her, Ryder went still.

"Complex case like that," the detective continued, "the physical evidence takes up lots of containers. Not so much for the paper reports, though. They fit in one box." The man covered a yawn with his hand. "Maybe I should go find myself some coffee." He shot them a lopsided grin and started for the door. Then he turned. "If you'd like, I could arrange for a couple of uniforms to pack up your clothes and personal items from your hotel rooms and bring them here."

"That would be wonderful." Carina smiled at him.

Graham nodded and stepped out of the room, leaving the evidence box behind.

Ryder lunged for the container and ripped the lid from it. Carina leaped up and peered inside. Lots of file folders, as well as loose papers. A musty odor tweaked her nostrils. She wrinkled her nose but reached for a folder anyway. Ryder stopped her with a grip on her wrist.

She pulled away from him and glared. "If anyone has a right to see this evidence, it's me. This is about *my* family."

He lifted his hands, palms out. "I agree, and I'm going to need your help going through all this. But allow me to filter the material first. Please. There will be photographic evidence in here with crime scene images I'm fairly certain you don't want to have stuck in your brain."

Carina gasped and pinched her eyes tightly shut. "Of course," she breathed. "I'm sorry. Please scan through things before you hand anything to me."

"Even with that, this stuff could be hard reading for you."

She opened her eyes and met Ryder's gaze. "This needs to be done. Let's get to it."

An hour later, Carina's head was full of gut-wrenching facts, figures and timelines, as well as leads that went nowhere and theories that suggested possibilities but that, by the end of the investigation, had remained unproven. No wonder the case had gone cold. Whoever had shot her parents and taken her had left next to no forensic evidence behind. The micro-scopic examination of her parents' lives had revealed nothing remotely suggesting a motive for the crime.

Gazing over at Ryder, Carina shut the folder she had been reading and hugged it to her chest. "At least I can say if anything positive has come from studying these police investigation files, I now know that any skeletons in my family closet don't extend beyond a parking ticket my father hadn't gotten around to paying before he was killed, and my mother's addiction to gourmet chocolate."

"True enough." He offered a faint smile. "But we have the address of your old home. That will be one of our next stops."

Carina slapped the folder down on the tabletop. "If there's no useful evidence from the police investigation, I don't know what clues could possibly remain in the house after fifteen years."

"Maybe not clues." Ryder fixed her with a steady look. "Maybe—"

"Memories." Carina finished the statement for him. Her voice trembled. Did she want to remember such a horrific experience? Probably not, but if she wanted to survive to raise her son, she had little choice but to try to fill the blank spot in her mind.

A knock sounded on the door and Carina jumped like a startled cat. Her heart pounded and her fists clenched. Really, she needed to get hold of herself. But in these circumstances, retaining equilibrium was easier said than done.

"Everything all right in there?" The detective's voice filtered through the door.

Ryder snatched up the file folders and papers that were currently on the table, tossed them back in the box and affixed the lid.

"We're doing fine," he said as he sank into his chair.

"Glad to hear it." Graham stepped inside and closed the door. He snapped his fingers. "Ha! Here's where I left that box. I was worried I'd mislaid it."

Carina stifled a soft laugh behind her hand, and Ryder grinned.

The detective grinned back. "Your belongings are here in the male and female locker rooms, respectively. I'll take you there shortly, and you can clean up and dress. Special courtesy extended toward a brother who was injured in the line of duty."

The man nodded at Ryder, whose face went studiously blank. Carina's heart went out to him. The merest mention of the courage and sacrifice that he didn't recognize in himself was tender for him still.

"But first, I sense you have some information for us." Ryder's eyes fixed on the detective.

The man nodded. "Fingerprint evidence is back on the pair who tried to break into Ms. Collins's room."

"What fingerprint evidence?" Ryder's brow quirked. "They were both wearing surgical gloves."

A smirk grew on the detective's face. "The goon with the gun didn't wipe his brass. Nice fat thumbprint on one of the unexpended bullets. Goes back to this guy." He produced a sheet of paper from his pocket and unfolded it to display a mug shot. Basic physical characteristics—height, weight, eye color, et cetera—were listed below the photo.

"This him?" the detective asked Ryder.

"Hard to say." Ryder shrugged. "The eyes look right, but both the assailants were wearing spandex ski masks."

"Who is this person?" Carina reached out and tapped the sheet of paper. Would they finally start getting some concrete information that might lead to more answers?

"Name's Beau Bryant," the detective answered. "Usually hangs with a chunk of pond scum named Duane Miller." He produced another mug shot. "Recognize this guy?"

"Same answer as before," Ryder said. "But the height and build listed on both mug shots fit the guys I saw."

Graham huffed. "Likely it's them. They're low-level muscle for organized crime in the state of Oklahoma."

Carina's lungs clenched as if all the air had been sucked out of the room. It was bad enough to think someone was trying to eliminate her for personal reasons. How had she become a mob target?

Ryder gazed at Carina. Her face had gone chalk white. Why would the mob be after her? That made no sense...unless the investigation into Carina's parents had missed the connection of one or both of them to organized crime.

Carina's eyes met his then darted away. Bright color drove the pallor from her cheeks. She was a smart woman. No doubt she was wondering the same thing about her parents. Not a feel-good moment.

"I think we need to interview the detective who was in charge of the case," Ryder told Graham. "Is he around?"

"Detective Cliff Sounder? He's retired, but still lives in Tulsa. I can give him a call. See if he'd be okay to meet with you."

"We appreciate it." He nodded at Graham.

"Yes, thanks for everything," Carina said, her tone sincere but brittle as thin glass.

The detective left with the evidence box and Ryder was left with Carina frowning at him.

"Why would we need to interview the detective who handled my family's case when we've already seen the reports?" she asked. "Isn't that a waste of time?"

Her voice held a growl, but Ryder couldn't take her attitude personally. She was afraid, with good reason. And now fresh suspicion had been thrown onto her family's integrity, just when she'd felt settled in her mind about them.

Ryder nodded and offered a small smile. "It's possible we won't find out anything new from Sounder, but we very well might. What makes it into written reports needs to be either cold, hard facts or at least logical assumptions or lines of inquiry suggested by those facts. The detective's gut feelings and impressions often go into personal notes or get filed away in the back of the investigator's mind, but don't necessarily make it onto the official pages."

The tension around Carina's mouth faded. "All right, then let's go see this guy."

"I hope we can do it over breakfast." Ryder patted his midsection. "I'm hungry."

"Me, too." Carina smiled, and her golden eyes lit up.

Ryder's heart expanded as if the sun had beamed down upon him. There wasn't much he wouldn't do to keep seeing that expression on her face.

Rein it in, buddy.

He'd only known the woman and her son for a day and half, and he was already thinking like a besotted oaf. Letting his feelings become personal was a great way to lose his focus and get her killed. No way could he let that happen. If she didn't survive physically, he wouldn't survive mentally. So what if his emotions took a hit when this was over and she walked away? At least he would know that this time he'd preserved a life that bad guys had wanted to steal.

The door opened and Graham stepped inside. "Sounder jumped at the opportunity to talk to you. The lack of closure in the case has always weighed on him. Let's get you down to the locker rooms so you can freshen up and change. The meet's all set up for forty-five minutes from now at a little mom-and-pop café up the street."

"You read my mind—or rather, my stomach." Ryder laughed. "I was just telling Carina that I was hoping for a breakfast meeting."

The detective grinned and shrugged. "What can I say? Cops think alike."

Ryder's smile wavered and faded altogether as he followed Graham and Carina out of the conference room. There was no such thing as an honorary cop, was there? He'd resigned from the force, but so far, he'd consistently been treated as a colleague here in Tulsa and in Argyle. Was there a message in that?

It was hard to shrug the question off in the men's locker room, an environment so familiar to him, where he took a quick shower and changed his clothes. The jeans and button-down shirt he put on weren't exactly the casual suit he'd worn daily as a detective, but he'd be more at ease if the surroundings and activity didn't feel so natural. He didn't *want* to feel at home here, but he did. How was that for fine irony?

Ryder connected with Carina outside the locker rooms. Faint dark smudges under her eyes betrayed her tiredness, but she looked lovely in a short-sleeved, green-and-white top and dark blue jeans. A small purse not much larger than a slice of bread hung at her side from a long strap that wound around one shoulder and led to the bag under the opposite arm. Her thick hair, still damp, was caught back in a ponytail. The style emphasized her rich amber eyes and striking features. His heart did a little *ka-bump*.

He dredged up a studiously casual smile. Hopefully, his reaction to her didn't show in his eyes.

"Ready to carry on?" he asked.

"Ready." She nodded and they headed upstairs.

As a courtesy precaution by Graham, a pair of uniformed officers escorted them down the block to the café. They bade the uniforms goodbye at the door and stepped into a cool interior furnished with chipped tables, faded seats and a scarred countertop. Homey, not classy. A good place. The atmosphere was relaxed with a buzz of friendly conversation, and inviting with odors of fresh coffee, cinnamon rolls and bacon.

A stocky man with a head of thick gray hair waved at them from a booth toward the rear of the long, narrow dining room. Ryder touched Carina in the small of her back to get her attention. He allowed her to precede him to the spot.

Here and there, he received and returned nods to uniformed officers and plainclothes detectives enjoying a filling start or possibly conclusion to their day, depending on their shift rotation. This was a cop hangout for sure, and apparently word of who he and Carina were and why they were here had gotten around. Typical. Police culture was like a small town when it came to the speed with which juicy gossip traveled…and in lots of other ways, too. Did he miss it? He wasn't ready to answer that question—even to himself. Maybe especially to himself.

Ryder slid into the booth seat next to Carina and opposite the man they had come to meet. A cup of coffee steamed on the table in front of the retired detective. The waitress arrived immediately and took Carina's and his drink orders, left them menus, then hustled away.

"Cliffton Sounder." The retired detective offered a meaty paw to Carina and then to Ryder. His shrewd brown-eyed regard returned to Carina. "You probably don't remember me, but we spoke several times soon after you were found in the park. You were a cute, gangly little kid, but you've grown into a lovely young woman."

The old-fashioned courtliness brought color to Carina's cheeks. "I'm a mother now…and a widow."

Sounder's expression sobered. "I'm sorry to hear you've had another major loss."

"I'm doing okay." She nodded. "Getting on with my life, until someone started trying to take it away from me anyway. Ryder's been a Godsend to thwart the attacks."

"Graham filled me in on that." The retired detective turned his attention on Ryder. "I'm honored to meet the guy who survived the bomb attack on the SWAT team in OKC."

Heat crept up Ryder's neck. Why did people act like he was some sort of hero when all he'd done was survive the blast that killed everyone else? He'd been as helpless as the rest of them when the bomb went off. Why had he been spared? He hadn't figured that out yet. Maybe he never would.

Ryder opened his mouth to speak but was relieved of the responsibility because the waitress arrived to get their orders. They took care of that business then he leaned toward the retired detective.

"One question has come to the front burner since we've become reasonably certain about the identity of the pair of goons who went after Carina at the hotel. I'm sure Graham told you about that, too, when he set up this meeting."

Gaze wary, the older man nodded.

"In your gut, outside of the formal report," Ryder went on, "was there the slightest whiff of a connection between her parents and organized crime?"

Next to him, Carina sucked in a faintly audible gasp. She probably hadn't been anticipating the question asked so bluntly. He didn't glance at her but kept his focus fully on Sounder.

The man held Ryder's stare steadily. "None whatsoever, and we tore their lives apart."

A deep and definite sigh came from the woman next to Ryder. He turned to her, and she met his look with a flicker of a smile. Her relief was understandable on one level—no innocent person wanted to believe their family was involved with the mob. But if Sounder's gut feeling was correct, the blessing was mixed because the organized crime connection became another dead end.

The waitress returned to their table with mugs of coffee for Carina and Ryder and a plate of bacon, eggs and hash browns for the retired detective. The savory smells drew a low rumble from Ryder's empty stomach.

The waitress grinned. "The other orders will be up soon," she informed them and then withdrew.

"Let's get our breakfasts out of the way—" the detective waved his fork at them "—and then we can talk."

Sounder dug in while Carina doctored her coffee with cream and sugar. Ryder sipped his black. The waitress was as good as her word, and Carina's and Ryder's food arrived a few minutes later. For a while, the only sound was silverware against crockery, chewing and swallowing. The plain, hot breakfast hit the spot. A few minutes later, Ryder wiped a dab of egg from his mouth with his napkin and settled his eyes on Sounder, who had finished before them and was nursing his brew.

The man offered a thin smile. "Okay, back to business. I don't mind telling you this was the strangest case I ever worked on. Somebody gains access to a house on a quiet, residential street—no sign of forced entry—then shoots the parents and grabs the seven-year-old kid, leaving no witnesses or forensic evidence behind except the bullets. And those led nowhere. No ballistic matches in the system and—"

Sounder quieted as the waitress arrived and refreshed their coffee.

"The kid goes missing," the retired detective continued once she was gone. "No whisper on the streets as to where she's gone or why she's been taken. Even the FBI are wringing their hands. Then—boom!—the kid turns up wandering around a local park, still in the same pajamas she was wearing when she was abducted, a cocktail of drugs in her system, and with no memory of what happened or where she's been all this time." The man raised his hands in a helpless gesture. "Frustrating is what it was—and still is." Sounder fixed his eyes on Carina. "Are you sure you don't remember any—"

"I'm sure!" The two words burst from Carina in a mini explosion.

Ryder reached out and wrapped his fingers around her hand under the table. She squeezed back as if hanging on for dear life. Sounder's tone had been almost accusing.

Ryder glared at the retired detective. "What are you implying? We came here for plain speaking. Spit it out."

The man leaned closer to them, returning his glare. "You want the only gut instinct I kept to myself? This awful thing that happened wasn't about the parents." He turned a flat, hard stare on Carina. "It was about you, Ms. Collins."

NINE

"About me!" Carina gaped at the retired detective.

Next to her, Ryder snorted. "What on earth could a seven-year-old kid get up to that would draw the attention of a stone-cold killer, much less the mob?"

"That, my friends—" Sounder held up an admonishing finger "—is the million-dollar question. If I knew the answer, the case would be solved."

Carina turned her head toward Ryder. He met her gaze with a tight-lipped frown.

"I have got to remember." Her voice emerged in a hoarse whisper through taut vocal cords. "We need to do what you said—go to the house where my family lived at the time."

Ryder nodded at her. "We'll go back to the police station and get our things. I'm sure they'll arrange for us to get back to your SUV at the hotel."

They paid their bill, thanked Cliffton Sounder, and took their leave of him.

At the police station, Detective Graham saw to it their belongings were returned to them, including Ryder's pistol. Fifteen minutes later, they climbed out of a patrol car under the shade of the canopy in front of the hotel entrance. Even at this early morning hour, muggy heat weighted the air.

Carina's shoulders slumped and her eyelids drooped in the stuffy atmosphere. She hadn't had nearly enough sleep last night and no rest at all from the constant tension since this deadly business had started. Not to mention she had arrived in Argyle already tired from the work of packing up and moving, as well as the emotional stress of dealing with her aunt's opposition to the move.

The patrol car drove away from them and Carina looked up at Ryder. His attention was everywhere but on her as his head swiveled while his eyes scanned the area. Her skin prickled like ants crawled over her. How she hated that such vigilance was necessary. How thankful she was that Ryder was there to provide it. And yet, she was honest enough with herself to admit the gratitude was tainted with a hint of resentment. Not against him. Against the situation. Independence had been the goal of her move—a goal that was now utterly thwarted.

"I should call my aunt and see how Jace is doing," she said.

He nodded. "What are you going to tell her?"

"As little as possible."

"Okay. You can make the call as soon as we get on the road. We're going to move out toward your SUV, and I want you to stay as close to me as you can."

Carina's heart *thudded* in her chest. "You think we might be attacked here?"

"I think we need to be vigilant wherever we go. Once we get in the SUV, I'm going to perform evasive maneuvers to make sure we're not being tailed. Ready to move?"

He looked down at her with a smile that didn't reach his wary eyes. She nodded then followed on his heels as they crossed the parking lot. Her mouth grew drier with every step, but they reached the vehicle without incident. As she passed the front bumper on her way to the passenger side, she allowed herself a deep breath. Out here on the sunbaked pavement, it was like breathing in a sauna, but soon she would be inside the vehicle with the air conditioner running.

"Stop!"

Ryder's sharp bark froze her in place. She gaped back at him. Face washed white, he was staring at the driver's-side door.

"Run! Right now!"

His tone lashed her and she didn't wait an instant. She took off, sprinting as fast as she could manage between and around vehicles. Close behind her came the slap of Ryder's feet on the tarmac. They pounded past the bulk of a full-sized van and—

Whoosh-boom!

The blast slammed her chest against the side of another SUV. Pain splintered through her rib cage where it met unyielding metal. Then she bounced backward and sprawled to the ground, dragging her elbows on the pavement. Pain splintered through her head where it met the ground, but her thick ponytail softened the impact. Ryder's heavy body plopped on top of her, smooshing her flat and driving from her lungs what little breath remained in them.

Shrieks rent the air as car alarms triggered in surrounding vehicles. A sharp stench of ozone and burning rubber swirled around them while metallic objects and other debris rained down, pinging against vehicles with a clatter like hailstones. Ryder jerked then slumped across her. Had he been struck by something? Hard to imagine he wouldn't have been hit, since his bulk had shielded her from the shrapnel.

Carina gripped his shoulders. "Are you okay? Please be okay."

Had she spoken those words out loud or just mouthed them? The ringing in her ears rendered her deaf to her own voice.

Ryder stirred and raised his head. His eyes were wide and his teeth were bared, as if gritting them against pain. He lifted himself to his hands and knees and moved away from her.

"We've got to get out of here," he said.

She read his lips more than heard the words.

"Shouldn't we wait for the police to arrive?" There, she'd faintly made out the sound of her own voice. "And an ambulance. You're hurt."

He shook his head. "Not badly, I don't think. You?"

"Scrapes and bruises. Maybe a bump on the head." She ordered her muscles to bring her into a sitting position. Her body grumbled but obeyed. "Yes, I believe I'm fairly whole." A warm trickle down her left forearm said the scrape on that elbow was bleeding, but considering what could have—should have—happened, she had nothing to complain about.

"Good." Ryder nodded. "We've got to get out of the area while our enemies are uncertain whether we survived."

"But—"

"Now!" His stone-cold stare halted protests on her tongue. "We'll make for the tree line at the back of the parking lot, staying low between the cars and out of sight as much as possible. Once we're past the trees, we're going to sprint as far as we can before we call a cab."

"I'm game," she said.

But was she? Her heart was racing and a lump clogged her throat. There was no better name to dub that lump than stark terror. But she couldn't allow fear to paralyze her. She had to do whatever needed to be done to stay alive until she could return to her son. Would that moment ever come?

Ryder's expression was set. Implacable. Yet the eyes that met hers held warmth. Caring. He lifted a hand and his rough palm cupped her cheek. Her fear receded and she leaned into his touch.

"Let's go," he said. "I'm armed, so I'll lead and make sure the way is clear."

Carina nodded. He removed his hand and she felt the loss. What should it tell her about her growing tenderness for Ryder that she would follow this man anywhere? She dismissed the question and raised herself into a squatting position behind him. He drew his weapon and headed out.

Scuttling in a crouch between the cars, they reached the back of the lot where a thin grove of poplar trees separated the hotel property from a strip mall. Behind them, shouts and screams signaled people's reactions to the bomb and its aftermath. As they emerged on the other side of the tree line, Ryder stopped and obstructed her path with an outstretched arm.

Red spots on the back of his shirt betrayed where sharp-edged debris had struck him, and there were scorch marks, too, where hot fragments had settled. His jeans didn't show the damage nearly as much, but there were a few scorched spots there as well. Her heart skipped, but at least no foreign objects protruded from his flesh, and he wasn't spurting blood. Still, he should go to the hospital to get checked out and have his wounds disinfected and dressed.

Ahead of them, people were vacating the mall parking lot by vehicle and on foot. Some were fleeing the commotion and possible danger. Others were moving toward it, curiosity overwhelming their fear.

Ryder skirted the edge of the row of trees until they reached the back of the strip mall, out of sight of the nearby busy street. Sirens were approaching. He tucked his gun in its holster and grabbed her hand, then they took off running along the alleyway behind buildings. Many blocks passed under Carina's feet and her lungs labored in the steamy air. Rivulets of sweat ran from beneath her hair and down her torso.

At last, Ryder slowed them to a walk then stopped underneath the awning of an electronics shop. Passersby awarded sidelong looks to their sweaty, panting dishevelment, but no one paused to speak to them. After all, except for their unusual attire for a workout, it wasn't a strange leap to think they were joggers.

Gasping, Carina doubled over and planted her hands against her knees, partly to keep them from buckling.

"Sorry…about that," Ryder said, also huffing a bit, but not nearly as badly as Carina.

She waved away his apology but declined to waste a molecule of precious oxygen with speech. At last, she raised herself, breath still coming in deep inhales, but without squeaky gasps now. She'd considered herself reasonably fit. Time to revamp her exercise program if— no, *when*—she was able to give a moment's thought to something so mundane.

"Tell me again why we ran from the professional help that was on the way?" she asked.

"We didn't run from the cops or the medics. We got out from under surveillance by the bad guys. That bomb was set off by a remote control held by someone within sight of your vehicle."

Nausea rolled through Carina's middle. She swallowed. "How do you know the bomb was set off manually?"

"The timing of the blast. Let's keep moving, and I'll explain."

He led the way across the street and Carina fell in beside him. No one in the area appeared to be paying them any attention, yet Ryder's vigilance was obvious in the slight swivel of his head as his gaze swept their environment.

"They wouldn't have set the bomb on a timer," he continued, "because they'd have no way of knowing when we would return for the vehicle. And if it had been wired to the ignition or a pressure plate under the seat, it wouldn't have gone off until we got in or when we started the engine. The bomb didn't detonate until we were running away—a clear indication that it took a few seconds for the person with the remote to realize we weren't going to get into the vehicle and decide to push the button."

Carina mulled his words and at last she nodded. "Makes sense. But how did you know the bomb was there?"

"I didn't *know* it was a bomb, but…" His voice trailed away and, though he shrugged, his face was tense. "Let's go in here and get a few things."

He led the way into a pharmacy. Blessed coolness enveloped Carina, and she was grateful for the detour into air-conditioning, but he wasn't going to get away with half an explanation. They stopped in front of a selection of bandages and antiseptics.

Carina wound her fists in the sleeves of his shirt and turned him to face her. "Finish what you were going to say."

His eyes dropped and he sighed. "I noticed the light coating of dust along the bottom side of the door on my side had been smudged, as if someone had rubbed against the underside of the vehicle. Bomb was the first thing that leaped to mind, and—" his throat visibly constricted "—I panicked. Running was all I could think of to do."

"You didn't panic." She put her hands on either side of his chin and captured his gaze. Pain and shame looked back at her. Not new and fresh, but old and lingering. His survivor's guilt in spades. "Listen to me, Ryder Jameson. You may have felt panicked—who wouldn't in that situation?—but you didn't lose yourself to fear. Far from it. Do you know what you did, you beautiful, brave man? You saved both of us. This time, you beat the bomb."

This time, you beat the bomb.

The words rang through Ryder like peals of a bell. The echoes jarred loose all kinds of knots in his psyche. Without a second thought, he wrapped his arms around Carina and drew her close. She fit so nicely, so naturally, against him, and she didn't resist but leaned into him with a deep sigh. Like coming home.

A chuckle rumbled in his chest. "Beautiful? I don't think I've ever been called that."

She lifted her head and grinned up at him. "Handsome doesn't alliterate well with brave, so deal with it."

"I guess I'll have to. Thank you." But thanks didn't begin to cover it. A fundamental shift had taken place inside him and he was going to need time to process the change. Just not this moment. "Let's grab a few things here and then find some place to doctor ourselves up."

"I still need to call Aunt Althea." She stepped away from him and unzipped the small bag slung over her shoulder.

Ryder released her and nodded. "I'll make our purchases while you do that."

She wandered away, phone to her ear, while he selected a few medical supplies. His back stung from sweat getting into the burns and cuts he knew must be there. He'd need to change his shirt after the wounds were dressed, but he'd dropped their small luggage bags when they'd run from the explosion. Happily, the pharmacy carried a rack of company logo T-shirts. He found one in his size and took the items to the checkout counter. Carina joined him there.

Carrying the bag with their purchases, he guided her toward the front door. "Everything all right with your aunt and Little Bit?"

She nodded without a smile. "I didn't mention the trouble from last night or this morning. Just told her we're still investigating, and I'll be in touch again later today."

"I'll book us a ride." He stopped near the entrance, pulled out his phone and opened the needed app. "We'll hole up in a seedy motel in a neighborhood where I can pay cash and register as Mr. Smith, with no record of you. Should have done that last night, but I underestimated our opposition." He wrinkled his nose. "Plus, I didn't want to expose you to that environment."

"No second-guessing." Her tone didn't allow argument. "We've already decided that's a waste of time."

"Right." He offered a lopsided smile as he entered their pickup information into the app.

Half an hour later, they were in a shabby part of town that clearly made their driver nervous. Ryder had the man let them out in front of a dilapidated gas station with bars on all the windows. As their driver whooshed away, he led Carina several blocks up the street until they came to a run-down motel with weeds and cracks in the parking lot cement and a sign advertising rooms by the hour, day or week.

"Wait out here in the shade of the eaves. I'll only be a moment registering as a single occupant under an assumed name. I don't want the attendant to see you."

Carina nodded with no comment and took up a position in the shadows. Checking in went without incident. Soon they were ensconced in a down-at-the-heels motel room. The furnishings were threadbare, and the place smelled musty, but they were out of sight in an untraceable location.

Ryder washed and dressed the bloody scrape on Carina's elbow and examined the small bump on the back of her head. She assured him she'd been experiencing minimal pain and no blurred vision. Likely no concussion, then, but he'd keep an eye on her anyway. Then he gingerly removed his shirt. The fabric had already stuck to some of the wounds. His long hiss as he pulled the cloth free was echoed by her gasp at the revealed cuts and burns.

"Sorry for the mess," he said, easing his weight onto a rickety chair. "But I'll need you to disinfect and dress the wounds."

"You put yourself between me and hot metal raining from the sky. I think I can manage a little first aid." She got to work.

Ryder clamped his jaw tight against outcries as the antiseptic was applied, but he couldn't entirely control flinching muscles. What did she think about the old scars on his arms and shoulders? The one on his left bicep, where a shard of metal had sliced to the bone, was pretty ugly. At least his torso was fairly clear of old scars. His helmet and tactical vest had absorbed the majority of the shrapnel from the bomb at the warehouse, but the multiple impacts had fractured most of his ribs, which resulted in a punctured lung. His legs had taken a lot of hits, too. Those wounds had needed the longest to heal, requiring intensive physical therapy to rehabilitate the damaged muscles, ligaments and tendons.

"There you go," Carina said at last. "Any open wounds are cleansed and covered, and the abrasions are disinfected. There were a couple of singed spots in your hair, too, but your head seems pretty much intact."

"Good to know." Ryder let out a brief laugh as he rose and put on his new T-shirt. "I shouldn't freak people out too badly now when they see me."

"Right. We *need* to go to my old house as soon as possible." She gnawed her lower lip. "What if the people who own it now won't let us in?"

He laid a hand on her arm. "We have to believe they're going to cooperate. If necessary, I'll enlist Detective Graham to help persuade them."

"We should call him and let the authorities know we're all right."

Ryder shook his head. "Not yet. Right now, we need to stay under the radar."

"Okay. I trust your judgment. Give me a minute." Carina started tapping on her phone. "I'm going to look up the location of the house and see what I can find out."

Ryder waited, studying her intent face. This morning's excitement had disheveled her hair in the most attractive way. Strands of it had worked free from her ponytail and framed her striking face.

"You're not going to believe this." She lifted her head and grinned at him.

The smile shot him right in the heart. He could look at that smile every day, all day long. She was speaking, but the words didn't register.

"Ryder, are you paying attention?"

"Say what?" He shook himself.

"My old home is on the market," she said. "We can arrange a showing right here on the realty app."

"Do it."

A few minutes later, they had an appointment secured for early afternoon. She showed him the confirmation screen on her phone then sank onto the edge of the bed as if her legs wouldn't hold her up. She'd gone sheet white.

Ryder's breath caught, and he went to one knee in front of her. "Are you all right?"

She stared at him, wide-eyed and breathing in shallow gasps. "I don't know. Suddenly, I'm more terrified of going to my childhood home than I've been this whole time we've been dodging one attempt on my life after another."

"I'll be with you every step."

"I know, and I'm so grateful." She gripped his hands.

The seconds stretched out impossibly long as her gaze melted into his. Ryder's heart thumped against his ribs. Millimeter by millimeter, he closed the gap between them. Her warm breath bathed his face. Only a paper-thin width stood between his lips and hers.

Suddenly, she inhaled a sharp breath and leaned away. "I'm sorry. I can't do this."

Ryder stood and stepped back, schooling his face not to show the disappointment searing through him. *Dumb, Jameson. Really dumb.* This woman was going through a horrifying situation. The last thing he wanted to do was take advantage of her emotional state. He had to embody strictly business from now on.

Too bad his heart had lost all good sense.

"Don't misunderstand me," she said quickly, her words practically tripping over one another. "I meant I can't do this right *now*, not that I never could. I can't trust my emotions at the moment, and I don't want to mistake my current dependency on you for something else. Something more…" Her voice trailed away as her eyes pleaded with him for understanding.

A tiny smile budded on his face. This was a wise woman, as well as honest and brave. He'd happily take *not never* and hope for the moment she would say *now*.

TEN

Had she really almost kissed Ryder? Why did she feel disappointed that she hadn't allowed the moment between them? Had she fallen for this guy already? Maybe an emotional attachment wasn't so strange when he'd saved her life umpteen times. But that was exactly what she didn't want—a relationship based on her need and dependency.

The questions niggled in the back of Carina's mind like an itch she couldn't scratch as she gazed through the taxi window at the home where she'd lived with her parents seemingly eons ago. She barely remembered the gray Craftsman-style house. Or maybe back then the color hadn't been gray. Green perhaps? And had the place looked so run-down when she'd lived in it? No, surely not. The whole neighborhood appeared to have deteriorated—that was, if she could trust her memory, which was the big question.

Carina squared her shoulders. Mulling over relationship issues would have to wait. They needed to stop whoever was trying to kill her before they succeeded. If that meant she had to face her fear about trying to remember what had happened in this house, then so be it.

She turned toward Ryder, who sat beside her in the back seat of the vehicle. "Shall we get out and walk around the yard while we wait for the Realtor to show up and let us in?"

He answered with that half smile of his that did strange things to her insides. "Might not be approved procedure realty-wise, but I don't see anything worrisome in the environment."

"You think it's safe?"

"No guarantees, but we can't sit here all day." That heart-stealing half smile again.

Carina turned away from him to look out at the scraggly lawn. "Let's go."

She opened her door and stepped out onto the curb. Muggy summer heat gripped her in a tight fist. At least the outside temperature might explain a little of the perspiration that suddenly coated her skin. But not all of it. Raw nerves played a big part.

Only birdsong disturbed the quiet. The neighborhood looked deserted. Probably because everyone was at work this time of day. A toddler's three-wheeler sat on a nearby lawn.

Carina's heart panged. How she missed Jace. He would love something like that. When this was over, she'd buy him one and teach him how to use it. Or maybe Ryder would— *Stop that!* When this was over, there was every probability he would move on to whatever life had in store for him next. He wouldn't be renovating his mother's house forever.

"Ready?" His voice came from beside her.

"As I'll ever be," she answered.

Behind them, the taxi pulled away as they trod onto the lawn. The grass was long enough to tickle her bare ankles above her sneakers.

"If I remember correctly," she said, "the backyard was a lot bigger than this postage-stamp-sized grass in the front."

"From here, it looks like the back is fenced in."

"It wasn't when I was little. I spent a lot of time out there. We had an awesome swing set, which was a big draw for all the neighborhood kids." Her lips curved in an involuntary smile. "What do you know? I *do* have pleasant memories of this place."

"Good. Things are starting to shake loose."

"But I have no idea if anything from the time of my lost memories will pop out."

The sound of an approaching vehicle brought Carina's head around. Next to her,

Ryder stiffened then stepped between her and the green sedan that pulled up to the curb and stopped. From the driver's seat, a woman with short brown hair waved and smiled.

"The agent, I'm guessing." Carina touched Ryder's arm.

The muscles were tense beneath her fingers, but the woman got out and announced her identity as Karen Briggs, Realtor, and the tension ebbed.

Ms. Briggs stepped over to them, a broad smile lighting her plain, pleasant features. The middle-aged woman was dressed in crisp, light-colored slacks and a floral-patterned blouse, and had stylish pumps on her feet. Ryder introduced Carina and himself and shook the agent's hand.

"What do you think?" The woman nodded at the house. "Needs a little tender loving care, but it's built to last," she went on without allowing an answer to the question. "Three bedrooms, one and a half baths. Perfect for a lovely couple like you two starting out."

At the phrasing about a couple starting out, Carina snuck a peak at Ryder's profile, but his expression remained bland. Her own heartbeat had done a little skip. Did that mean she wanted the words to be true?

"Shall we go inside?" Ms. Briggs asked.

"By all means," Ryder answered.

Now that the moment to enter had come, Carina's mouth went too dry to speak. She followed the Realtor up the steps onto the pillared porch that extended across the front façade. Ryder brought up the rear, no doubt scrutinizing the environment with hawk eyes like she'd seen him do before.

Ms. Briggs unlocked the front door, stepped through and then held the door open for them. Holding her breath, Carina stepped over the threshold. A great emptiness met her. In front of her, a set of carpeted stairs led to the second story. To the left was an average-sized living room. Beyond that, a dining room filled the space. There were no furnishings, just bare rooms surrounded by walls coated in old paint and peeling wallpaper, but the woodwork was typical, sturdy Craftsman and in decent shape.

Sunlight beamed in through side windows, but the light coming through the picture window in the front was muted due to the overhanging porch. The atmosphere was stuffy, though a low hum indicated a central-air unit was attempting rather unsuccessfully to beat off the Oklahoma heat.

"Like I said—" the Realtor nodded around the interior "—a little TLC, and you'll have a cozy, well-built home."

"How long has it stood empty?" Carina finally found her voice.

"This time, about a year."

"This time?" Ryder prompted.

The woman's lips flattened before she dredged up a businesslike smile. "The house has changed hands four or five times in the two decades I've been a Realtor in this area, but I assure you, each time the owner's move had nothing to do with the quality of the house. Why don't you go ahead and do a walk-through? I'll meet you out on the back deck to answer any questions you might have."

"Sounds like a plan," Ryder said.

Ms. Briggs proceeded across the carpet in the living room, then her low heels clickety-clacked across the hardwood on the dining room floor and out of sight, presumably through the kitchen. A creak followed by a soft smack suggested a door opening and closing at the other end of the house.

Carina inhaled a shaky breath and let it out slowly as she stepped into the living room. She closed her eyes. Where had the furniture been? A soft-edged picture emerged of a sofa bracketed by matching end tables and lamps, a pair of easy chairs, a square coffee table, a few family photos and a framed Bible verse on the walls. But mostly she remembered the warmth and the laughter.

"I used to play board games with my parents on the coffee table," she said softly, her heart squeezing in on itself. "The police report said this is the room where they…were shot."

A lump clogged her throat. Ryder's hand fell gently on her shoulder and she reached up to grip its firmness. Her eyes eased open and she scanned the carpeting. No trace of what had occurred there. What had she been expecting? Old bloodstains? Of course, the carpet must have been replaced, probably more than once in the past twenty years.

"It's disturbing to stand here where happiness and tragedy collided," she told Ryder.

He squeezed her shoulder. "Where was your bedroom?"

"Upstairs. We need to go there, but I'm terrified. That's where the killer found me."

"It'll be like this space, Carina. An empty room. And I'll be with you."

"Thank you."

Steeling herself, Carina turned and trod to the stairway. She looked up into the darkness and shivered. Ryder flipped a switch and the darkness turned to light.

A strangled laugh left her throat. "There's a

metaphor in that action somewhere about what a difference a little light makes."

"Let's go see if we can find some more metaphorical light." Ryder echoed her soft laugh.

Carina led the way up the stairs, their passage awakening a few creaks and groans from the old boards. When they reached the top, she headed for the second bedroom on the left, directly across from the bathroom.

"This is it," she said as she stepped through the open door and looked around.

Like Ryder had said, nothing was here now but an empty room. To her right, the entrance to the closet was flush with the rest of the wall. The recess jutted out into the hallway and met the bathroom closet, creating the effect of shortening the upstairs corridor, but maximizing the space in the rooms. Light poured in from two windows—one opposite the door and one on the outside wall that looked out over the backyard. Like she'd done in the living room, Carina closed her eyes and imagined the area as it had been.

A twin-sized bed hugged the wall at right angles to the door but opposite the window that overlooked the backyard. A lampstand and lamp stood sentinel next to the bed, and a pearly-white dresser with pink-scalloped trim occupied the wall farthest from the door. Her beloved and much-used pink dollhouse with its lavender-and-white trim perched on the floor beyond the bed. And, of course, the whole room had been decorated princess-style. A smile spread across her lips. At seven years old, she'd been oblivious to how clichéd the décor was and supremely happy with her little domain...until that night. The smile died.

She opened her eyes. "He found me in the closet. When I started hearing all those scary noises downstairs, I hid."

"This is a memory now? Not the recurring dream?"

"I believe that's what actually happened." She nodded. "I think I need to get into the closet and curl up in the corner like I was that night."

"I'll be right here."

She sent him a tremulous smile. "You keep saying that, and I keep needing to hear it. Thank you. Here goes."

She pulled wide the closet's sliding doors and found the space smaller than she remembered it—but at that time she'd been much smaller herself. An empty clothes pole ran from one end of the closet to the other, and above that an empty shelf board ran the length of the space, offering additional storage. The carpeting didn't extend into the closet, and scuffed boards lay bare to the eye.

"I hunkered down in the furthest corner from the bad noises." She pointed. "I was not at all a brave child—kind of nerdy and bookish. Still am, for that matter, and still not all that brave either."

"You were a *child*, not expected to face down armed killers. Most adults couldn't do that. And nerdy and bookish can be an awesome superpower. But I beg to differ about the brave part. You're about the bravest person I've ever met."

"Says the guy whose career expected you to run *toward* danger, not away from it."

Ryder frowned. "The difference isn't the amount of courage, it's the training."

Carina shook her head at him. "A person needs both to do the job you had, but we can debate the point later. Right now, it's going to take a bunch of guts for me to step into this closet, hunker in the corner and imagine that night again. And, yes—" she held up a hand "—I know you're here, and am I ever glad of it. Thank you again."

"You're more than welcome."

Did his tone contain a special tenderness? Whatever it was, warmth filled her and her knotted stomach settled. Without another word, she stepped into the closet, assumed her position and closed her eyes.

Almost at once the dream came—only she was awake. The shouting below, the gunshots, the sound of footsteps on the stairs, a hulking creature flinging wide the closet doors then reaching for her. She gasped and shuddered, goose bumps coating every square inch of her body.

Then the man spoke. Neither in her dreams nor in her memories had he ever done so before. This was a new recollection.

Carina cried out, her eyes popping open. She reached for Ryder, who she found crouching in front of her, and gripped his arms. Her gaze locked with his.

"You remembered something," he said. "What is it?"

"Almost nothing," she gasped. "But maybe something." Her pulse fluttered. "My kidnapper asked me a question. He said, in this growly, mean voice, 'What did you do with the rocks, kid?'"

"Rocks? What rocks?" Ryder leaned closer to Carina.

"I don't know." She shook her head. "Or maybe I do. I have to dig the memory out. Not from the part *after* the kidnapping. That is still wiped from my brain. This is a regular memory, but I need to put it together because it's been so long."

She leveled herself to her feet, stepped around him and went to the window overlooking the backyard.

"What is it?" Ryder followed her to the window.

As she'd told him earlier, the yard below was more than twice the size of the front yard. The area was empty, however—no trace of her beloved swing set. Not that he'd expected it to still be there.

"Look!" Carina pointed to a corner of the yard where a large oak tree spread shade across the lawn. "Two days before I was kidnapped and my parents were killed, my dad finished building a tree house for me, and it's still there—or, at least, some of it is. Looks like it's falling apart now."

Ryder leaned closer to the pane of glass and made out boards stretched symmetrically across thick tree branches. Some of the planks were missing, but the structure still resembled a tree house.

Carina turned from the window and hurried toward the door. "I need to get up there. This memory I'm looking to flesh out has something to do with me sitting in my brand-new tree house like a princess in a castle."

Ryder strode after her. "Hold on, Carina. You're going to need help climbing up. It looks like any ladder that might have existed is gone. And someone needs to be nearby to catch you if one of those rickety-looking boards collapses."

She stopped at the head of the stairs and pivoted to him. "I trust you with all of that, but this is something I have to do."

"Understood." He nodded, his throat thickening as he gazed into those earnest amber eyes.

She couldn't know how much her unwavering trust meant to him. Actually, *he* hadn't known how little trust he'd come to have in himself since the bombing in Oklahoma City. Not that the feeling was the least bit rational. As counsellors had assured him time and again, he couldn't have known about the bomb any more than anyone else on his team, and he couldn't have saved anyone no matter how much he wished he could have. But the guilt had been eating him up—until Carina came along with her courage and her faith, despite the nightmare she'd lived through in her childhood and the terrors she was facing now.

God, please help me to be worthy of her trust.

Ryder followed Carina as she hurried down the stairs and strode without pause through the living room, dining room and kitchen to the back door. They stepped outside onto a small deck and found the Realtor pecking at her phone. The woman lifted her head and smiled at them.

Carina practically skidded to a halt with a small "Oh" falling from her lips. Ryder barely stopped himself from bumping into her. He managed to suppress his own exclamation of surprise, but in the excitement of the impending breakthrough, he had forgotten the woman's presence as Carina obviously had as well.

"What do you think?" Ms. Briggs asked with a bright smile.

Carina didn't answer but charged ahead down the deck steps and onto the lawn.

"Give us a minute," Ryder told the Realtor as he hustled past.

Crossing the yard toward the tree, his skin prickled. Were they being watched by hostile eyes? How could they be? To see over the fence, any observer would need to be stationed on the second floor of one of the surrounding houses. Not likely, but not out of the question either. He scanned the homes overlooking them, but not so much as a curtain twitched.

What about the Realtor? He glanced over his shoulder at her. She'd gone back to pecking at her phone. Nothing about her suggested assassin. Besides, the woman's appearance matched the photo on her realty website, so she was likely not a threat. No, his attack of nerves was all wrapped up in anticipation of whatever revelations might come.

Carina reached the tree trunk and Ryder stepped up behind her. Hands fisting and then releasing, she stared up into the thickly leaved branches. He followed her gaze. The weathered boards of the old tree house peeped back at him through random bare spots between the foliage. So close but so far away, when even the lowest tree branch jutted out beyond reach.

"Boost me up," Carina said. "If I can pull myself onto that first branch, I can climb into the tree house."

Without a word, Ryder leaned his back against the sturdy trunk and offered his cupped hands, fingers entwined. Hardly sparing him a glance, Carina placed a sneaker-clad foot into his palms, gripped his shoulders tightly and lunged upward. Her hands left his shoulders as she ascended, and her entire weight rested briefly in his care. For a moment, his biceps strained, then she grasped the thick branch and her weight left him entirely. Lithe as a young monkey, she pulled herself to a seat above him.

"What are you doing?" The agent's sharp voice came from a few feet away.

Ryder turned his head to find her glowering at him.

"This is not safe," the woman continued, looking upward and frowning. "I'll have to ask you to come down, Ms. Collins. Liability issues."

Carina paid the Realtor no attention as she stood on one branch and reached up to the next.

"Don't worry, Ms. Briggs," Ryder said. "We won't hold anyone responsible for anything that happens, but we have to do this. This is personal and immensely important."

The woman planted her fists on her hips. "I still don't like it."

"I remember!" Carina called down.

A thrill jolted through Ryder. He stared upward to find Carina squatting on one of the tree house boards and staring at the alley beyond the back fence.

"What do you remember?" he called back.

"I'll tell you as soon as I check something out. Help me down."

She was already lowering herself to him. A

moment later, she was dangling by her arms from the lowest branch. Her toes hovered several feet from the ground. She could jump and be fine, but he'd rather help.

Ryder grabbed her around her slender waist and set her on *terra firma*.

Face bright, eyes distant—her reality anchored somewhere in the past—she whirled and took a stride toward the house. However, the Realtor planted herself in Carina's way, halting her progress.

"Stop," the woman said. "What is going on?"

"We'll explain soon," Ryder told her as Carina dodged around the woman and continued toward the house. "Just go with it for now."

Then he, too, bypassed the openmouthed woman and hurried after Carina. She was already charging through the back door. Ryder increased his speed to a run and caught up with her as she traversed the living room. He followed her up the stairs and back to her childhood bedroom. Carina knelt on the carpet at the edge of the closet opening. Her gaze seemed to be searching the bare floorboards of the closet's interior.

Ryder knelt beside her. "What do you remember?" He repeated his question from moments ago.

She met his gaze, a golden fire in her eyes. "It was fall. School had started and the teenager my folks hired to walk me home and stay with me until they got off work settled into the dining room with her notebooks and textbooks. But I ran right outside and climbed into the tree house. It was my first day to play in it. And I saw a man."

"A man? In the tree house?"

"No." She rolled her eyes with a grin. "In the alley. Running past."

"What did he look like?"

"Big. But that assessment may be relative because I was little. Other than that, I don't know. He was wearing jeans and a dark sweatshirt with the hood up, covering his head. No way could I see his face because I was looking down from above. And he had his hands stuffed in his pockets. At least, he did until he tripped over my kick scooter. Then he pulled his hands from his pockets to catch himself as he fell."

"Your scooter."

He must sound like a parrot, but the details seemed so off the wall. How was any of this relevant to Carina's childhood tragedy?

She huffed. "Remember, there was no fence back then, and the day before this I must have left the scooter under the shade of the tree, partially sticking out into the alley. When the man fell, my hair stood on end. Sure, I cared if the guy was hurt or not, but mostly I was worried he might complain to my parents. Mom and Dad would scold me for being careless with my things. Not only because I'd left the scooter outside overnight, but because the thing was a hazard to others."

"Parents are unreasonable like that." Ryder smirked and Carina smiled.

"Horrors!" She went on in a dramatic tone. "Maybe I'd even get grounded. This wasn't the first time I'd forgotten their instruction to keep my stuff in the yard, not the alleyway where people and cars sometimes passed. But the guy just grunted, muttered something under his breath, got up and ran on. Was I ever relieved!"

Ryder chuckled. "I well recall those *oops, I'm in for it now* moments from my own childhood."

"You got that right." She nodded then sobered. "But here's the important part. I noticed something must have fallen out of his hoodie pocket. There was a little black drawstring sack on the ground. I figured I'd better get down there pronto and see if I could catch the guy to give it back to him. I scrambled out of the tree house, but I was too late. The man was nowhere to be seen."

"What was in the sack?"

"Rocks."

"Like gravel or pebbles or landscape rocks?"

She shook her head. "Glittery stones. Lots of them. Irregular shapes and various sizes. Some were as small as peas. Others looked like pinto beans. But a couple of them nearly filled my palm. The color varied, too—from mostly clear to smoky gray. I knew right away what they were."

Ryder's heart began knocking against his ribs. "Gemstones?"

"No, quartz."

"What?"

"At the time, I was certain I was right. My dad and I used to go on hikes and he'd taught me about rocks. The glittery ones attracted me the most. I was something of a magpie back then and collected shiny things. Dad told me quartz was pretty but not valuable because it was common. Didn't matter to me. I brought home the best of the rocks we found. When I saw the ones in the sack, I *really* wanted those. They were the best ever, so I tucked them away in my secret place with my other treasures and didn't tell a soul."

Ryder's gaze scanned the interior of the closet. "I take it your secret place is somewhere in here?"

"Under a certain loose floorboard. If I can find it…" Her voice trailed off as she began pressing against the narrow, scuffed-wood strips. "It doesn't look like the flooring has been replaced in here."

"Let's hope not." Ryder began helping her with the task. "Here!" he cried out.

A board toward the back wobbled slightly under the pressure of his palm. Carina crowded up against him, the fresh strawberry scent of her shampoo gracing his nostrils.

"Let me," she said. "I used to use a nail file to pop the board, but my fingernails will have to do the trick today."

Ryder grasped her hand as she reached for the loose board. "No need to risk breaking a nail." He pulled his pocketknife out, opened it and slid the edge of the blade into the narrow crack. The board section popped up and he removed it.

Carina pressed in, and Ryder yielded to her. It was her right to look first. She leaned over the dark opening with her phone flashlight shining down into the space.

"Is the bag in there?" Ryder asked.

"It should be because all my old things look to be here, just jumbled around, so I can't make out individual items until I pull them out. At least I don't see any spiders." A shudder rippled her shoulders.

She reached into the opening and came out with a round brass medallion with scraps of ribbon attached to it. The medal looked new, but the cloth had mostly rotted away.

Carina flickered a smile at him. "My school award for coming in third in a sprint race."

She set the object aside on the floor and reached in again and again and again. Several chunks of quartz rock joined the medal, then a few pieces of sleek black mica.

"From your walks with your dad?" Ryder asked.

"Told you I was a magpie."

She laughed as she brought another stone out and showed it to him. It was an irregularly shaped rock, about the size of a baseball, that had been cut in two. The outside of the rock was dull gray, but the interior glittered with crystals.

"A geode," she said. "Dad bought it for me in a souvenir store when he was on a business trip." Her eyes suddenly shone with moisture. She reached into the hole and came out with a tarnished silver charm bracelet. "Mom bought me this. It was too big for my wrist. Kept falling off. So I put it in my secret place to keep until I grew up."

Her bottom lip quivered and she tucked it between her teeth. Her stare fell away as tears wet her cheeks.

Ryder's heart cracked in two like that geode. "You're certainly grown up now." His voice had gravel in it. He reached for the bracelet. "Here. Let me." She allowed him to unclasp the bracelet and then fasten it around her wrist. "Perfect fit."

Her eyes devoured the dainty piece of jewelry. "I can't believe I forgot these things were here."

"Why would you give trinkets another thought after the trauma you went through?"

She sighed and looked up at him. "Thank you. For everything. Especially your understanding."

"My pleasure."

His chest was clamped in a vise. He could scarcely breathe. If only it wouldn't be selfish to reach out and pull her close, but he'd almost indulged his errant feelings this morning. He wasn't about to abuse the timing again.

"Is the sack in there?" Ryder blurted out the words—anything to regain proper focus.

Carina broke eye contact. The disconnect shook him, but at least he could draw air into his lungs now.

She shone light into the space under the

board. "There's nothing more here." She swiveled toward him. Her gaze was wide and stricken. "The bag is gone."

"You know those weren't quartz rocks, don't you?" Ryder's tone was low and tight.

She nodded. "With twenty-twenty adult hindsight, I do."

"They must have been uncut diamonds. Stolen, most likely."

"No wonder the man invaded our home, killed my parents and kidnapped me. His question—'where are the rocks, kid?'—makes total sense now." A spasm passed over her face. "While he had me, I must have told him where to find the diamonds, and he came back and got them. But I don't understand. If he already ripped through my world and took everything he wanted back then, why is he trying to kill me now?"

ELEVEN

"It was all my fault." The words bled from Carina's lips.

Her parents were dead because she'd been a foolish child, hiding her prize, oblivious to danger. She stared at the dull gray wall of the police station conference room. How long had she been sitting, semicomatose, while Ryder spoke with Detective Graham? How had she even gotten here?

As if viewing life from a dreamlike distance, vague recollections trickled through her brain—of Ryder slipping the Realtor a few twenties as an apology for taking up her time, and then getting them a ride to the station. Floundering in the swamp of her thoughts, Carina had been useless for anything, including talking to the detective when their arrival was greeted with a flurry of activity. Apparently, cops all over the city had been looking for them after the car bombing and it became clear no one had been inside the vehicle.

A firm but gentle hand came to rest on Carina's shoulder. Wrenched back to the present, she blinked up at Ryder.

"I know *exactly* how you feel," he said.

A lump clogged Carina's throat. She could hardly argue with that statement, given his own struggles with survivor's guilt. Only her guilt was a bit more tangible than that.

Ryder crouched on his haunches in front of her chair, bringing his face near hers. He clasped her hands in both of his. Her icy digits craved his warmth, and she curled her fingers around his palms

His storm-blue gaze melded with hers. "You were a little kid, behaving innocently. There is no way you could have realized what was going on. Nothing was anyone's fault except the lowlife who chose his actions."

The knot in Carina's stomach eased the smallest bit. The shock and the guilt were far from gone, but dealing thoroughly with toxic reactions would have to wait. Ryder took a seat beside her, his solid presence a tether to her ping-ponging emotions.

She looked to Detective Graham, standing across the table from them, eyeing her gravely.

"Was there a diamond heist in my neighborhood at that time?"

"Yes. I was just telling Ryder about it."

"Tell me, please. I'm ready to listen."

The detective nodded. "Approximately forty-eight hours before your family home was invaded, a jewelry store about a mile from your house was robbed of an extremely valuable shipment of uncut diamonds—by a man wearing a hoodie and a monkey mask."

Carina shuddered. "Ugh, a mask."

"Ties in with the guy in the car taunting you in Argyle," Ryder said.

The detective nodded. "Certainly seems to. The suspect fled the store in a stolen GMC Yukon, but a security guard managed to shoot out one of the tires. The vehicle was abandoned half a mile from the robbery, and we deemed the suspect to be on foot."

Carina leaned forward and planted her elbows on the conference table. "That's when the guy ran through my back alley."

"It would appear so." The detective took a seat across from her. "He was apprehended a few blocks beyond your house."

Carina gasped. "You caught him? Then how—"

Ryder placed a hand on her arm and she bit back further words.

"We caught the guy, and we were sure he did it," the detective continued. "But without the diamonds, we had no evidence other than that the crime fit his MO for theft and violence, and he happened to be in the neighborhood."

"Did his MO include a connection to organized crime?" Ryder asked.

Graham nodded. "Then, for sure. Now?" The detective shrugged. "We thought the mob cut him loose when he got nabbed and sent up for another crime."

"Apparently not." Ryder snorted. "Mob thugs don't show up at someone's hotel room door when there's no connection whatsoever."

"Let's get back to the time of the diamond heist," Carina said, her teeth practically on edge.

"Right," Graham said. "We brought the guy in for questioning and held him as long as we could, but eventually we had to kick him loose."

"Didn't you follow him, hoping he'd lead you to the jewels?" Ryder asked.

"We did. The surveillance team tailed him to his apartment and staked him out." The detective's lips pressed into a thin line and his gaze darted away from them.

"Bu-u-ut?" Ryder drawled the prompt.

Graham's eyes met Carina's. "If this is the guy who murdered your parents and kidnapped you, then he must have had a way to leave his place without being seen."

"What's his name? Do you have his location?"

"His name is Milton Trainer, and we know where he is." The corners of the detective's lips tilted upward the smallest degree. "Trainer was released from prison a few months ago and is currently on probation. We're bringing him in as we speak. And someone else."

"Who?" Carina asked.

"His cousin Everett Hicks is—*was* a pharmacist. Lost his license a while back for illegal dispensing."

Carina's heart bumped against her ribs. "Someone like that would have been able to administer the drugs that were found in my system when I suddenly showed up in the park."

"You think Hicks could have been an accessory two decades ago?" Ryder said.

"Connects the dots." The detective nodded.

Ryder frowned. "But why would Trainer and Hicks want to eliminate Carina twenty years after the fact?"

"That's one of the things we want to find

out," Graham said. "You two are welcome to view the interrogations."

"Thank you." Carina put all her heart and soul into those two words. Was she about to be free of the death threat and get final answers to that long-ago tragedy?

Thirty minutes later, she was in a cubicle of a room, clinging to one of Ryder's hands and staring through one-way glass into a cramped space occupied by a scarred table and a jittery man sitting in a chair across from a pair of empty chairs. Graham had told them they were going to start with the ex-pharmacist because they deemed him the weaker link. Judging by the way the wiry, balding, fifty-something man kept squirming in his seat, scratching himself like he itched all over and darting his gaze here and there, that assessment seemed accurate.

Graham and a female detective entered the room. Hicks went rigid and his prominent Adam's apple bobbed. The pair of detectives took seats and Graham slapped a thick folder onto the tabletop. The ex-pharmacist jumped up, staring at the file as if it were a rabid animal about to bite him.

"Sit down!" the female detective barked.

Hicks sank into his chair, staring at the cops with eyes wider than quarters. "Wh-what is this about?" His words emerged in a croaking stammer.

The detectives didn't answer. Instead, they proceeded with the preliminaries of notifying the suspect that the interview was being recorded and stating the Miranda warning. Maintaining innocence of anything, Hicks declined an attorney.

At last, Graham placed his hands atop the file and pinned the ex-pharmacist under a steady stare. Carina crept closer to the glass. Ryder wrapped an arm around her shoulders and she leaned into him. The pleasant outdoorsy scent of his shampoo wafted to her, overlaid by a faint antiseptic smell from first aid at the dive motel. The tension in her gut eased a slight degree. Like he kept telling her, she was not alone.

"Why are you trying to kill Carina Collins?" the detective demanded.

"Kill? I've never tried to kill anyone. Never. Never." He punctuated his words with shakes of his head like a dog shedding water.

"But you don't deny you know Carina Collins," the female detective said. "Or Carina Willis, as she was known twenty years ago."

Hicks froze and went stark white. The man stared, wide-eyed, toward the one-way glass, as if facing an oncoming train.

"Twenty years ago," Graham said, "a shipment of uncut diamonds was stolen and then lost by the thief. Two days later, in a nearby neighborhood, an innocent set of parents was murdered and their seven-year-old daughter was kidnapped. Do you know anything about that?"

Hicks abruptly went rag-limp, head and shoulders sinking onto the table. He mumbled something unintelligible.

"Speak up," the female detective clipped out.

The ex-pharmacist lifted his head, a smile flickering on and off like a faulty light bulb. "It's over. Finally, it's over."

"Go on," Graham prompted.

"It wasn't me… I mean I didn't steal anything, kill anyone or kidnap a kid. Let's be clear about that."

Graham tilted his head. "How about you tell us what happened?"

Hicks licked his lips, eyes darting from one detective to the other. "My cousin brought her to me."

"The little girl?" asked the female detective. "Carina?"

"Yes." The ex-pharmacist nodded. "She was absolutely catatonic and utterly mute. From fright, I think. Her psyche had simply shut down."

A sheen of sweat suddenly coated Carina's body. She still didn't remember any of this. Only the feeling. That part was clear and sharp. Abject terror. Her pulse rushed like a torrent in her ears, her mouth turned stone dry and her breathing went shallow and swift. Blackness edged her vision.

"Hang in there." Ryder's voice rumbled low and calm. "I've got you."

Right. This was two decades later. She was an adult now. Carina schooled her breathing and the roaring of her pulse receded.

"Milt wanted me to get her to tell him where the diamonds were," the suspect continued. "I didn't want to help him. Not with a child. But I knew he'd kill me if I didn't. Kill her, too. So I tried different medications. She had an allergic reaction to one of them, went into anaphylactic shock, and we nearly lost her." The guy's Adam's apple bobbed again. "But I pulled her out of it and insisted we wait—let her stabilize—before we continued. Milt was *not* happy, but I…ah—" The man blinked and sucked in an audible breath. "Yeah, it was me. I got him to see sense."

Ryder's arm across Carina's shoulders went

rigid. "The guy's lying, or at least leaving something out."

"Lying about the allergic reaction or about something else?"

"I don't know."

They fell silent, as their words were drowning out Hicks's continued story.

"...got a result about twelve hours later. The kid blabbed. Milt went to collect his jewels, but the cops were all over the place, so he couldn't get access to the house."

"What happened next?" Graham asked.

"We had to wait until the police left the crime scene. Let me tell you, Milt was nervous as a teenager on a blind date that you-all would find his diamonds, especially when you took your sweet time on the evidence collection. At least, I knew the kid's life wasn't in danger until he verified the loot was where she said it was. He said I had to keep her sedated until then, though."

The female detective snorted. "Would your choice of sedation drug have had a side effect of wiping the memory, like a roofie?"

"Indeed, it would. In fact, it was that class of drug I used. Very carefully dosed because of her age." The guy's tone implied pride in his skill.

Carina's stomach curdled. She'd always believed her amnesia was due to hysteria, and that one day she might remember. Perhaps her memory blank had started that way, but at least some of it was chemically induced—a part of what had been done to her, not solely an internal self-defense mechanism indicating an inability to cope with events.

Detective Graham leaned over the table toward the ex-pharmacist. "Why should we believe any of this? Milt is sitting in the next interview room. You know he's going to deny it all. Do you have any proof of his involvement?"

"Sure do." The man sat straight and squared his shoulders, like self-respect had suddenly returned. "Video and audio recording of Milt questioning the kid. Yeah, he's wearing a mask, but you'll have no trouble matching the voice to him griping about the loss of his diamonds and bragging about the way he shot those poor people. I kept the recording for insurance, in case my cousin decided I was a loose end. You can have it now. I need this thing off my chest, and he needs to be locked up with the key thrown away."

The detectives rose and exchanged glances.

"What you've told us should about do it," Graham said.

Hicks's expression turned furtive, like a

hunted animal. "I know I'm not going to get out of this free and clear, and I've got it coming, but don't stick me in the same prison as Milt."

"That'll be up to the judge," Graham said.

"Put in a good word for me, will you? Tell him the kid's alive because of me." The ex-pharmacist's voice went shrill. "That should mean something."

Carina pressed her fingers to her lips.

A low growl rumbled from Ryder's chest. "Like he's owed a pat on the back now?" he muttered.

The female detective set the file on the table. "Explain."

Hicks's head bobbed in vigorous nods. "I saved her, all right. You folks finally finished at the house, so Milt went to get his rocks. He said, if the gems were where she claimed, he didn't have any more need for the kid and could dispose of her. I couldn't stomach murdering a child, so I turned her loose in the park." Hicks stuck out his pointy chin. "My cousin was plenty mad at me, but he got his loot, so that helped his attitude. Plus, I promised him the kid wouldn't remember a thing, so he only beat me up a little bit."

The detectives exchanged another glance.

"Okay," Graham said. "All this will be noted

in your statement. You sit tight while we go see good old Milt."

The detectives left the room and Carina turned to face Ryder. She fisted the shoulders of his T-shirt in her hands. "I don't want to listen to the interrogation of Milton Trainer. I don't want to hear him talk about what he did—or try to deny it."

Ryder nodded, gaze tender. "I was going to recommend you not subject yourself to that. I wasn't sure you'd listen to me."

She inhaled a huge breath then let it out slowly. "But I do want to see him. Just look at him through the glass. I want a real human face to put beneath the terrible shadow of that hoodie."

"Good." Ryder smiled and tucked a stray strand of hair behind her ear.

The soft touch sent a tingle through Carina. Did she care that his presence was growing as necessary and natural to her as her next breath? Not right now she didn't.

He grabbed her hand and tugged her toward the door. "Let's go to the next observation room and expose a monster."

Ryder studied Carina while she studied the man who had torn her family apart and terrorized her twenty years ago—the man who was now the best suspect for a player in the attempts on her life these past few days. Ryder had read Hicks as sincere in denying involvement in the current attempts on Carina's life. That meant Trainer had a different accomplice. The person's identity would need to be uncovered before he'd feel easy about Carina's safety. Right now, he was more concerned for her sanity. This moment had to be beyond hard.

Her face was nearly bloodless, and her jaw muscles twitched as if she were gritting her teeth. No doubt she was. Rivers of fury and anguish had to be coursing through her. Yet her chin was high and her regard held steady. She was the picture of a woman facing down her worst nightmare with courage and grace.

"That's the man who terrorized me and murdered my parents?" She turned fierce eyes on Ryder. "He's husky, for sure, like plenty of guys. Not monstrous, like he is in my mind. And his face is so average-looking…except for the hardness in his eyes. Mostly, he seems tired and bitter. If I saw him on the street, I wouldn't cross to the other side to avoid him. I wouldn't even give him a second look."

The detectives entered the interrogation room. Carina gripped Ryder's arm and he put his hand over hers. The petite hand trembled slightly under his touch.

"I want to know why this man has been coming after me now," she said, "but I think that will involve what happened in the past. I don't think I can handle any more talk about that until I process what I've already found out."

"Understood," he said. "The detectives will find out why he's been trying to eliminate you after all these years."

But would they? Ryder didn't voice his skepticism as he ushered Carina from the observation room. A worn-out ex-con like Trainer shouldn't have the resources to send a professional hit man after someone, much less mob thugs. They were missing something, but he had no idea what it could be.

"I don't know about you," he said as they walked up the dingy cop shop hallway, "but I'm starving. Why don't we let the detectives do their thing while we wander over to that restaurant where we had breakfast?"

Carina nodded. "I don't know if I can eat, but I'm very thirsty."

They left the building, and muggy air weighted with vehicle exhaust odors met them as they stepped out onto the city sidewalk. Road traffic was heavy and noisy. Ryder scanned the environment but observed nothing suspicious. Still, he placed himself between Carina and the street and kept her near the buildings as they walked along. If she noticed the protective strategy, she didn't say anything about it. Head down, she moved along beside him somewhat mechanically, as if on autopilot.

They reached the café without incident and went inside. The place wasn't as busy as it had been this morning. Different people occupied the booths and tables, but the law-enforcement-watering-hole vibe remained. Multiple cop eyes observed their entrance and followed them to a booth. Ryder exchanged nods with a few of them. No one seemed to recognize exactly who he was, but cops knew cops as instinctively as crooks knew cops, and their postures visibly relaxed. Ryder relaxed also. Carina was safe in here.

The waitress showed up, pen and pad in hand. Ryder ordered the meat loaf special, but Carina asked only for a big glass of iced tea with a side of water.

"She'll take the meat loaf special, too," Ryder told the waitress.

The woman left and Carina glared at him.

He offered a small grin. "When you inhale that hearty food smell right under your nostrils, you might change your mind about eating. But if you don't, I figure I'm hungry enough to do the honors myself."

A tiny laugh spurted from her. "Okay, you win." Her body slumped. "Mostly, I'm so tired I could sleep for a week."

"I hear you. We haven't had decent rest for a couple of nights now."

Had it only been two days since they'd entered each other's orbits? If he didn't know better, he'd say they'd become close friends. At the very least, he'd be lying to himself if he didn't admit to *wanting* to know her at that level. Maybe even deeper than that.

He observed her strong and lovely face as she sipped iced tea through a straw. His heart turned over. This was a woman he could love. A woman with whom he could share a future. Did she feel even remotely the same way? What had changed inside him that allowed him to think thoughts of a future—of permanence? Two days ago, he'd been shuffling through the motions of life, not knowing and largely not caring what the next day might bring.

Her gaze lifted to his and time became irrelevant. Who knew such a cliché could be so true?

"What?" she said at last, breaking the connection with a sharp blink.

"Thank you," Ryder said.

Her eyebrows pulled toward each other. "What are you thanking *me* for? I wouldn't be alive right now without you."

"Maybe I've participated in keeping you physically alive, but emotionally, even spiritually, you've brought me back to life."

"Only God can do something like that."

"True, but you've been the human agent. So…thank you."

Her amber eyes sparked and shot a tingle through Ryder.

"When this is all over, would you—"

His blurted question was cut off by the arrival of their food. Steaming ceramic plates holding meat loaf, green beans, and mashed potatoes and gravy were deposited from the waitress's hands onto the table in front of them. He'd been right about the hearty food smell. His mouth watered. Probably better if he stuffed his face with meat loaf and fixings rather than put his foot in it by asking Carina out on a date right now. Like she'd said, she had a lot to process, and he needed to give her space to do it.

Carina poked the meat loaf with a fork and brought a bite to her mouth. "Mmm," she hummed. "You were right. Maybe I can eat after all."

They shoveled the food in without another word. Ryder's heart buoyed. Sometimes silence between two people was uncomfortable. But this wasn't. Did that mean good things for the possibility of a developing relationship? Carina paused with her last bite of meat loaf near her lips, and Ryder met her sober glance.

"Just like that," she said.

"Like what? Meat loaf?"

Carina laughed and the musical sound resonated through Ryder's insides. But a frown followed and stilled him through and through. He laid his fork down and gave her his attention.

She tilted her head, and moisture gathered at the corners of her eyes. "Just like that, a twenty-year-old cold case is solved. I know what happened and why. I've got all this lovely hot food in my stomach, and yet I'm suddenly empty. Like the *not knowing* occupied so much inner space that uncovering the truth has hollowed me out."

"You're not feeling closure?"

"My parents are still gone, and my memories haven't returned. The pain and loss still lurk, but now there's guilt as well, that I played a part in what happened."

"An unwitting part." Ryder leaned toward Carina and she allowed him to cup one of her hands in his. "Over the past couple of days, being with you has helped me more with my inner struggles than any amount of counseling ever could."

"I'm glad of that." A faint smile curved her lips.

"Me, too. More than I can say. One thing that's finally registered in my thick skull is the futility of beating oneself up with regret. Most of the time an innocent mistake is no big deal and easily corrected. But once in a while the consequences are huge, totally blindsiding a person. And there's no fixing what happened. But " A lump thickened in Ryder's throat and he dropped his gaze from Carina's.

She squeezed his fingers. "What?"

Ryder peered at her through lowered lashes and gathered himself. The restaurant sounds—the buzz of voices, the clink of silverware on plates—faded into nothing.

"I've never told anyone this. Not even my department-assigned shrink." He swallowed against the lump. "I had a bad feeling about going into that warehouse the day of the bomb. Something was...off. Finding the location of the human traffickers had been too easy. I met the informant who passed along the intel. Briefly. The guy was jumpy."

"Wouldn't that be normal behavior for an informant?"

"Most of the time." Ryan nodded. "But this guy's fear seemed supersized. Like there was more going on than a typical exchange of money for information from a street rat. I've always had this—oh, I don't know what you might call it, but let's put it this way—a gift for reading people. Sometimes I contradicted other cops and even my superiors because of it. My colleagues started teasing me, and in the supposedly good-natured razzing, I was hearing notes of resentment from people I considered my friends. So that day I decided to keep my mouth shut about my doubts. Just trust the orders and carry them out. You know how things went from there."

He let out a snort and folded his arms across his chest. Classic defensive posture, but he couldn't help himself.

Scowling, Carina scooted out of her booth seat and slid into his, pressing him into the corner. She glared into his face. If a five-foot, three-inch person could intimidate a six-foot, two-inch person, she was doing it in spades.

"Tell me, Mr. People Reader, would your

boss have called off the raid because of your instinct?"

"I don't know. Maybe."

"But maybe not."

"Probably not. The powers that be were pushing for a big win in the human trafficking situation in our city."

"Then it sounds to me like there were plenty of factors at play with more than enough blame to go around. What were you saying about the futility of regret?"

Her words pummeled him with their truth, even as he fought the urge to kiss the mouth so close to his. Ryder turned his head away, but she gripped his chin and pulled it her direction.

"You're telling me, Ryder Jameson, that you suited up and followed your team into a situation you sensed more clearly than anyone else could be a trap. You did it because you were loyal to your friends and colleagues, and you were doing your duty. That sounds like raw courage to me. Now, I suggest you give God permission to help you forgive yourself for any way you fell short."

Warmth spread from Ryder's chest up into his face, relaxing stiff muscles. A smile trembled on his lips. "I will if you will."

"Deal." She echoed his smile.

Their behavior was gleaning attention from

nearby customers. But did he care? Not even a little bit. He'd take every moment he could get sitting close to this woman. What would he do if a return to normalcy and safety caused her to decide she didn't need or want him around anymore?

TWELVE

A ringtone sounded and Carina jerked, removing her hands from Ryder's warm skin. She huffed and leaned away from him while she dug around in her shoulder bag.

Her face heated. What must he think of her for presuming to lecture him? Sure, they'd made a connection. But at what level? Friends? Something potentially more? She didn't have time to sort out the nuances of a relationship right now.

Carina pulled out her cell and frowned at the screen. "The call is coming in from my aunt's landline. I'll let her know we'll be there as soon as possible. We have a lot to tell her, and I want to be reunited with Jace."

"Sounds like a plan." Ryder's gaze had gone cool and remote.

Carina answered the call and a male voice responded to her hello. What? Oh, yes, Frank.

It had been a while since she'd spoken with her cousin.

"You kept your promise to visit your mother," she said.

"Don't sound so surprised, cuz." Forced amusement barely masked a prickly undertone. "I see her as often as my job will let me."

Resentful excuses were normal with Frank. Time to change the subject.

"Everything okay with her and Jace?"

Several heartbeats of silence answered her. Carina went stiff, meeting Ryder's inquiring stare.

"That's what I'm calling about," Frank said at last. "Mom's busy with Jace and asked me to contact you. I think the kid's come down with some sort of stomach bug. Mom says you shouldn't come home. She can handle it. But I disagree. I don't know what you've got going on that's more important than caring for your son, but you'd better get here as fast as you can."

Her cousin's words turned a corkscrew in Carina's heart. Evidently, Aunt Althea had not seen fit to fill Frank in on the dangerous situation that had necessitated Carina's separation from Jace. The reason for keeping the information to herself was likely comprehensible only in her aunt's convoluted psyche. Carina had known leaving Jace with Aunt Althea would come back to bite her somehow, but her son becoming ill, and her cousin all but accusing her of neglect, hadn't been in any scenario. However, Frank's opinion of her mothering skills was beside the point. She'd have a conversation with him and her aunt at a later time.

"We'll be right there," she said.

"We? Probably should ditch the date. It's not pretty here." Frank snickered. "You'll put him off asking you out again for sure."

"Dating isn't even on my radar," she snapped in a clipped tone. *Thank you, cousin, for reminding me of the importance of standing on my own two feet.*

Did hurt flicker across Ryder's face? Surely not. His expression was attentive but impersonal. Exactly the way she wanted it to be. Didn't she?

"I'll see you soon," she told Frank and ended the call.

"Jace?" Ryder asked.

"My cousin says he's sick. I have to go."

"*We* have to go."

"No, please." She shook her head. "It's silly for you to come. I need to take care of my own sick child. The bad guys are in jail. You don't have to protect me anymore. The best thing you can do for me right now is stick close to the police station and find out what excuse Trainer gave Detective Graham for trying to kill me these past couple of days."

"That's important but—"

"No buts. I'm going to see my son. I'll call you later."

Carina scooted out of the booth and headed for the door. She really should pay for her half of the meal, but getting to Jace took priority right now. She'd make it right with Ryder later.

"Wait!" Ryder's voice trailed after her.

But she didn't wait. Now that the danger had passed, it was vital she reestablish her independence, and this was an opportune time to start. Besides, Frank was no doubt right about involving Ryder in caring for a sick child. He hadn't signed up for that particular challenge.

A cab was driving by as Carina stepped outside. She flagged it down and hopped inside. At least the vehicle's interior was much cooler than outdoors, but she was less appreciative of the odor of stale French fries overlaid by cheap air freshener. Carina gave the cabbie the address and then sat wringing the strap of her purse as the business area eventually gave way to residential streets.

At last, the cab slowed and angled to the curb outside Aunt Althea's house. Frank's Jeep Wrangler sat in the driveway in front of the closed door of the single-car garage where his mother kept her Volkswagen Jetta. The neighborhood looked quiet as usual with few cars passing and several sitting parked in driveways. A bulky blue SUV sat idling at the curb in front of a house a couple of doors down. The tinted windows didn't allow her to see inside. Somebody waiting for someone, no doubt. All very normal.

Carina chuckled at herself internally. Ryder's constant vigilance had rubbed off on her.

The cab stopped, Carina handed the driver the fare plus tip, and she hopped out onto the curb. Only last evening, with the sun dipping down beyond the houses like right now, she and Ryder had pulled up here in her SUV to drop Jace off. Now, her vehicle was toast—quite literally—and she was here, sans Ryder. So much had changed between that moment and this. The mystery of her past had been solved, and it was time to get back to the nitty-gritty of real life in the moment. Her son needed her, and she needed him. They were enough for each other, and she would keep telling herself that until she believed it.

Carina half trotted, half ran up the sidewalk and then climbed steps to her aunt's house. The front door was unlocked, as she'd expected it to be. Without hesitation, she burst through into the tiny foyer. The area was dim with no lights turned on, although her aunt had already closed the living room curtains, as she always did in anticipation of night falling.

"Aunt Althea!" she called. "I'm here."

No one answered her. Carina stilled her breathing and listened. The refrigerator groaned to life and the air handlers exhaled nearly inaudible breaths of cool air. No human voice or footfall broke in on the standard noises.

"Hello! Aunt Althea? Where's Jace? How is he?"

Still no answer. Had her son become so much worse that an ambulance had been called? Was everyone at the hospital? Carina's breathing stalled. Surely, if that were the case, someone would have reached her on her cell to let her know. Or maybe they'd left a note. The most logical place for that type of communication would be the dining table.

Heart hammering in her chest, Carina hurried across the living room and past the half wall separating that area from the dining room and kitchen. She halted just beyond the transition from carpeting to the hardwood floor of the dining room. Her gaze devoured the area. The dim glow of appliance screens revealed no one in the kitchen. Nearer at hand, Jace's high chair sat in its usual place by the dining table. No Jace in it, of course. And no note either. Carina reached for her purse to retrieve her cell phone then froze, gaping at the framed doorway that led from the kitchen into the laundry room.

A dark figure oozed out of the deep shadows into the dimness of the kitchen. The person was dressed in black from head to toe, and a hood framed the inky emptiness where the creature's face ought to be.

The scream that always in sleeping nightmares past had remained trapped behind clenched airways erupted from Carina's throat.

"Could we go a little faster?" Ryder urged his driver.

"Chill. I'm not about to have an accident. This is *my* car, you know."

Ryder sighed and sat back.

Traffic was not all that dense, and so far, they hadn't come anywhere near getting into an accident, but he couldn't force a driver to go faster than he was comfortable going. Fingernails biting into his palms, Ryder stared out the window as the scenery drifted too slowly past his window.

Now was not a good time to be at the mercy of an uber-cautious driver. Carina must have grabbed the last cab on their street, so he'd had to use an app to summon a ride. Waiting had cost him six minutes he wasn't sure he had. Ryder hadn't caught much more than the gist of Carina's conversation with Cousin Frank, but the guy had done a stellar job of pushing her buttons as only someone who had lived with a person knew how to do.

Maybe Ryder was overreacting and the danger to Carina had truly ended. He'd thank God if the worst difficulty facing her right now was her child's illness. But if Trainer and Hicks had the resources to pull off the sophisticated and resourceful attacks Carina had experienced, he'd eat the badge he used to have.

Ryder had read in Hicks that the guy knew more than he was telling about the horrible crimes twenty years ago, and Ryder's gut said that knowledge might be key to what was happening now. However, unearthing that information might depend on the interrogation skills of Detective Graham and his partner. Trainer probably knew the secrets being held back also. But Carina had opted out of that interview for understandable reasons, and Ryder's uneasiness had told him to stay with her.

Until she'd ditched him, thinking she was safe.

His fault.

Nausea swam through him. How would he live if she died because he'd kept silent, wanting to give her space to process life-changing revelations? He'd thought his presence would be enough protection while she got her mental and emotional bearings. He should have shared with her the depth of his reservations about Trainer and Hicks being the culprits currently wanting her dead.

Now, all he could do was try to catch up to Carina while he waited for Detective Graham to return the call he'd made the minute he arranged for his driver. Graham hadn't picked up the phone call—he was probably still interviewing the suspects—so Ryder had left a detailed message about Carina's and his current situations and what he needed to know.

At last, they turned onto the street where the aunt's house was located. On one side of the road, an elderly man was out walking an equally elderly-appearing dog. On the other side, a bulky blue Ford Expedition sat with its engine running. The man and the dog raised no alarm. In fact, the pair was already turning to stroll up toward a house. However, Ryder peered closely at the massive SUV. With the windows so darkly tinted, it was hard to say if anyone was inside, much less multiple people. Probably nothing, but he wasn't going to take risks.

Ryder's hand went to the pancake holster at his hip. His weighty Glock had blown sky-high with Carina's SUV, but he still had the lighter Shield pistol concealed under the bottom of his T-shirt. As the driver brought the vehicle to the curb in front of Althea's house, Ryder unsnapped the holster with one hand and let himself out of the car with the other. The vehicle drove away with more zip than the driver had displayed the whole ride here.

Fingers wrapped around the grip of his pistol, Ryder stepped toward the Expedition. He wouldn't pull the gun yet in case the occupant or occupants were innocent strangers. Walking over to have a word with the driver would be as aggressive as he would get. Unless the presence of this vehicle turned out to be less than innocent. Then things could get ugly fast.

Two steps into his approach, a blood-curdling scream rang out from inside Althea's house.

Carina!

Ryder's heart stopped then leaped against his ribs like a bull bursting through the gate. Forget the idling SUV. He whirled and raced toward the haven that had once taken Carina in—but now might be the snare that would take her life.

THIRTEEN

Carina stood frozen in place, pulse tap-dancing in her throat, gaze riveted on the dark figure. One of the dark man's arms lifted and the kitchen can lights suddenly blazed to life. Carina blinked and recoiled a step. The figure from her nightmares resolved into a smallish male wearing jeans and a hoodie—not terribly intimidating under the stark glow of light bulbs. Even if Milt Trainer had somehow escaped or been released from custody at the police station, this wasn't him. Entirely wrong body build.

"Who are you?" Her words choked out from a tight throat and clenched jaw.

The slight man swept the hood back from his face as he crossed the kitchen and stepped up to the dining room table across from her. Her stare met the golden-brown eyes so similar in color to her own, and a familiar fine-boned face grinned at her.

Carina's insides turned to water and then boiled. "Frank! What in the world do you think you're doing? You scared a decade off my life. Where's Jace?"

"Where he should be," her cousin said. "With my mother."

"Is he worse? Did she take him to the doctor?"

"She took him to the park and plans to stop at the grocery store before coming home. They won't be back for at least an hour. Jace is fine, little cuz. But you're not."

"What do you mean? You called and said…" Carina's voice trailed off as her glance fell to an object Frank had pulled from his pocket. "Why are you pointing a gun at me?"

"The gun will ensure your cooperation." Frank's eyes left her and fixed on a spot beyond her shoulder. "And your boyfriend's."

"My boyfriend?"

"Toss away your gun, Detective Jameson, and show yourself with your hands in the air. At this range, I won't miss your girlfriend even if you could get out a shot at me."

Ryder was here? He must have followed her.

Carina looked over her shoulder as a bulky object hit the living room carpet. Ryder's pistol. Then the man himself stepped out of the dimness of the foyer. Carina's heart leaped.

His sturdy figure was much more substantial and intimidating than her cousin's. Except, Frank had a gun and Ryder's hands were raised in surrender.

"I'm sorry," he said softly, his look tender upon her.

"No, *I'm* sorry."

What a prize idiot she'd been to run off without him. Her phobia against dependency hadn't served her well—or him, either. Then again, would they be in any different situation if they'd been together from the start? Neither of them had suspected Frank of anything.

Carina looked into Ryder's steady blue eyes and had her answer. Here was a strong man upon whom she *could* depend without fear of being dominated or manipulated. He'd never done either of those things throughout a whole gamut of intense situations. If she'd simply yielded and trusted in a situation where he was the trained expert, quite likely he could have steered them clear of the situation they now faced. Even now, that rocklike gaze assured her he'd do everything in his power to get them away from danger. But how that might work out, she had no clue. The weapon was in the bad guy's hands.

Carina turned and glared at her cousin.

"What do you think you're doing, Frank? This makes no sense."

"Have a seat." Her cousin motioned slightly with the muzzle of his gun. "You, too, hot-shot cop."

Sinking into a chair, Carina kept her regard fixed on Frank. Why had she never noticed the joy he took in intimidating others? His glee trumpeted from the grin on his face and the manic light in his eyes. Then again, she had never attended the same school as her cousin because he'd been a teenager at the time she'd moved into her aunt's home. When not in school, Frank had happily made a point of either being in his room or out with friends. To Carina's recollection, he'd never been around except for meals, which he'd shoveled in and then escaped again. A part of her could understand the behavior.

"It must have been refreshing for you when I came to live here," she said, faintly registering Ryder taking a seat beside her.

Frank kept his pistol firmly pointed in their direction even as his jaw dropped. "You totally get it. I shouldn't be surprised." Then his eyes narrowed. "At first, I was jealous of my mother pouring her time and attention on my needy little cousin, but it didn't take me long to appreciate the freedom her obsession with you gave me. At last, my every living, breathing minute was not regulated and supervised."

"Aunt Althea is a good woman."

"She is, but she's also a total control freak."

"She's afraid of losing a loved one. If she can wrap herself around us, she thinks we'll be safe. Like our well-being is her sole responsibility. She means well, but her fear makes her unintentionally take over the place of God."

Carina halted her rush of words with a gulp. Where had that insight come from? For the first time, as if in a burst of revelation, she saw her aunt's behavior with an eye of compassion rather than resentment.

Next to her, Ryder let out a soft grunt. "What does any of this have to do with you holding us at gunpoint, Frank?"

"Yes, and why have you been trying to kill me?" Carina asked. "It's been you all along, hasn't it?"

"Allow *me* to answer those questions." An unfamiliar masculine voice spoke from behind them.

Carina swiveled in her chair toward the unknown man. The newcomer was of average height and slender build and was dressed in a lightweight summer suit of expensive, tailor-made quality. She had never met the man before. But what was it about his lean face that seemed familiar? He might not be holding a gun on them, but a look in his eyes proclaimed he was more dangerous by far than the one who was.

Ryder seemed to snap out of a temporary paralysis and turned to the man with the jerky motion of one whose muscles had gone rigid. Carina looked toward him, and goose bumps cascaded over her flesh. With everything they'd been through, she'd never seen fear on his face like she was seeing now.

"Orlando Spinx." The man's name surged from the depths of Ryder's being. "On every cop's radar as the biggest crime boss in central United States."

Repulsion crashed through Ryder like a tidal wave. Carina and he could *not* be at the mercy of this evil man.

A soft and gentle hand closed over his forearm. Ryder slid a glance at his companion. Her stare was upon him. Did he see confidence there? Confidence in whom? Him? Yes, to a degree. But mostly she was telling him to trust God. How? Did he have any trust left in him? For her sake, he would try. But he'd also keep his eyes open for the slightest opportunity to turn the tables. If he lost his life, so be it, but Carina *would* be saved.

"Why is a crime boss standing in my aunt's living room?" Carina's tone was calm—conversational even.

"Excellent question, my dear." Spinx stepped closer and waved a hand at Frank. "Meet my son."

A heavy weight settled in the pit of Ryder's stomach as the blood left Carina's face. How could she not know of the relationship? Had she hidden this news from him all along?

Openmouthed, Carina swiveled her head to her cousin. "Franklin Kellman. I've never known you by any other name."

"The legal name change was Mom's doing, of course. She tacked her maiden name onto both of us." Frank scowled. "Didn't want anyone knowing her or my connection to the up-and-coming mobster she married in ignorance and then divorced in regret."

The weight in Ryder's core lifted. Carina hadn't known.

"And I was content with that state of affairs," Spinx said, "especially when I had no time for family. I needed all my attention focused on clawing my way up the organization's food chain. But then Frankie hit his teens and got curious about his father. He started looking for me, and I made sure he found me. Amazing how much my boy thinks like me when

I had no hand in his upbringing. Makes one meditate on the impact of nature versus nurture. But I digress into philosophy."

The smug superiority in the man's expression begged to be smacked off. Ryder's fists clenched then he forced them to loosen. He needed to play it smart and cool until his moment came.

"You never answered the question about why you've been after Carina?" Ryder forced the words out like bits of gravel though clenched teeth.

Spinx shrugged. "Simple. She wouldn't cooperate."

"Cooperate?" Carina's brows snapped together.

Frank snarled an angry word. "You're too stubborn to stay here where you belong so you could keep Mom's attention off me. You have no idea how maddening it is to receive multiple calls day and night over trivial things and constant begging for a visit. The nagging started every time you struck out on your own. First when you married, and then I could see it was going to happen again when you got a job away from Tulsa."

Narrowing his eyes, Ryder turned toward Spinx. "Why would you care about keeping little Frankie's mommy off his back?"

Frank's face reddened and he growled another curse, but Spinx shrugged.

"Simple," he said. "My son is brilliant with money. He's been setting up the slickest laundering scheme I've ever seen. I couldn't have him distracted from his vital work, and Althea has a gift for wearing people out."

Frank heaved a sharp laugh. "Dad and I are immensely practical. I've always done what I needed to do to keep Mom off my back."

"What did you do, Frank?" Carina's words were breathy and faint.

Ryder's skin prickled. What *had* her cousin done? More than try to kill her these past few days?

Spinx cleared his throat. "There are some excellent, nearly undetectable drugs that will simulate a heart attack in the healthiest specimen, and I know where to get them."

A keening wail came from Carina's throat as she bent over nearly double. Ryder laid his hand on her quivering back.

He stared daggers at Frank. "You killed her husband. Jace's father."

Carina's cousin shrugged, not a hint of remorse in his expression. "I grew up without a father in the house. It's not the worst thing in the world."

"But it's better with one," Spinx said. "Right, son?"

"For sure, Dad."

The pair grinned at each other, and Ryder's stomach turned over. These two deserved one another—in a maximum security prison, together for life.

Carina lifted her head, cheeks tearstained, and fixed stormy eyes on her cousin. She sniffled and cleared her throat. "Now you're trying to kill me so Althea will have Jace to raise and keep her occupied." Her eyes narrowed. "You're the one who terrorized me by following us in Argyle wearing a mask. And you lost your patience and tried to run me down at the convenience store. Everything else that required planning and resources, your father engineered."

Spinx clapped his hands together. "Frankie told me your brain wasn't all there, but I see you're quite smart."

"She's not that smart." Frank scowled, looking from his father to Carina. "I needed to keep you jumpy and scared, so I did the mask thing. And at the convenience store? Well…" He squared his shoulders. "Dad's taught me never to pass up a golden opportunity. If not for hero cop there—" he jerked his chin toward Ryder "—you'd already be roadkill, and

Dad and I would be on to the next big thing instead of wasting time with you today."

"If you've got big things going on," Ryder said, "and we're a waste of time, why don't you walk away and forget about us?"

Spinx and his son started laughing. Ryder tensed for that key moment of inattention. It didn't come. Frank kept his gun trained on Carina and Spinx drew a small pistol from his suit pocket and pointed it at Ryder.

"Good one," Spinx said, sobering.

"Trying to be helpful." Ryder rolled his shoulders in a shrug that also helped keep them loose for action. Though, with another gun in the mix, the opportunity for that had just gotten exponentially smaller. "So now you shoot us? Happy ending for you?"

"Not quite…or at least not here," Spinx said. "Can't have my ex-wife's home become a crime scene. It'll draw too much attention to the place. There's a gentleman outside in the Expedition who would like to take you somewhere private and finish what he started with Carina. My contractor is even doing you for free, Jameson. He bears a grudge. Let's be on our way." The man waved them forward with his pistol.

Ryder rose slowly. He couldn't allow this pair to get them to that vehicle where the contract killer waited. He glanced at Carina, who stood beside him. She was still blinking back tears. His arms ached to hold her, comfort her. But through her pain, the firm set of her jaw and the glint in her eyes assured him she would fight beside him to live.

All he needed was a plan.

Carina took a step, but her foot must have hooked on a chair leg because she cried out and fell forward, yanking the chair over on top of her. Plan? Who needed a plan when that aforementioned golden opportunity knocked?

Ryder flung himself to the side as Frank shouted and his gun fired. Grabbing another chair, he tossed it upward toward Spinx, but barely connected as the mob boss stutter-stepped in reverse, redness blooming on his belly. His son's bullet had met an unintended target.

Ignoring the pain and breathlessness from his abrupt collision with the unforgiving floor, Ryder scrambled underneath the table and shoved himself forward, plowing his head and shoulders into Frank's knees. Carina's cousin went down like a bowling pin. The gun blasted again. Glass shattered and an overhead can light blinked out. Ryder clawed his way up Frank's prone body and yanked the pistol from the man's loosened grip while the guy was dazed from the back of his head bouncing against the hardwood.

Now armed, Ryder rose into a crouch and whirled toward any remaining threat the wounded Spinx might pose. The mob boss was down, slumped against the coffee table, gripping his stomach with both hands and moaning. There would be no further danger from him.

"Behind you!"

At Carina's cry, Ryder spun as a scowling figure, familiar from that night in Carina's bedroom, stepped through the back door into the kitchen. The man's gun was leveled at the largest target. Him.

The boom of Ryder's gunshot echoed through the space as an invisible giant's fist slammed into his chest. He flew backward and landed on the floor, gasping for breath. An intense numbness spread through his torso. Not an echo of his shot then. Mr. Pro-Hitter's gun had spoken on top of his, and he'd taken a bullet.

He'd experienced violent puncture wounds from projectiles before. Shrapnel. He knew the drill. Adrenaline was keeping the pain at bay—for now—but when the pain hit, it would be bad.

Carina. Where was Carina?

Her outcries came to him, shrill but distant, like he was hearing her from the far end of a tunnel. Suddenly a flurry of other male and female voices buzzed urgently around him. Did he recognize one of them as an ally? Detective Graham?

His eyelids were weighted. Too much effort was required to keep them open.

More hustle and bustle. People messing with him. Why couldn't he swat them? Tell them to go away and leave him alone.

Then the pain attacked like a vicious animal with burning fangs. His body was shutting down. Good. He needed to let go. But a warm breath caressed his ear, tethering him to consciousness a few seconds longer.

"Ryder Jameson, don't you dare die on me. I love you!"

I love you, too, Carina, he answered. Or did he only think the words?

Then there was darkness and silence.

FOURTEEN

Carina scooted her chair a little closer to Ryder's hospital bed and studied his sleeping face. His thick, ebony eyelashes—the kind many women paid money to emulate—rested on high cheekbones. Finally, after two nail-biting days, his color had improved and he was breathing easier than he had since his wounding followed by intensive surgery. The professional killer's bullet had missed his heart by a whisker, and he'd lost a lot of blood. But the doc said if Ryder made it this far, the prognosis for recovery was good.

Thank You, God.

Several times over the past couple of days, Ryder had awakened briefly, dazed and groggy. He'd taken in a little water each time and then fallen back into a semicomatose state without acknowledging anybody or anything around him. Maybe he would wake up in normal consciousness soon.

A knock sounded on the door.

Carina turned to find Detective Graham poking his head into the room.

"Any improvement?" The detective responded to her gesture to step inside and came to stand by the bed.

"I think he's doing better," Carina said. "I'm expecting him to open those baby blues any minute and greet me like he's ready to rejoin the world."

"I'm with you on that." Graham studied Ryder with a furrowed brow. Then he turned to Carina. "I stopped in because I thought you might want to know Spinx's condition has been upgraded from critical to serious. Unless he takes an unexpected turn for the worse, he should make it, but they're not sure if he'll walk again with the way that bullet damaged the spinal cord. Once all the charges are filed against him, he's looking at multiple life sentences that he's likely to serve in a wheelchair. People are coming out of the woodwork to testify to his criminal activities now that it's clear he's in no shape to organize retaliation."

"Spinx is going down?" a deep voice asked.

Carina gaped at the man in the bed. His blue eyes gazed back at her, clear and sharp.

"You're awake!" She smiled at him.

"Do you think I'd sleep through the great

news that a major mobster is finally going to meet justice?" He started to chuckle but a grimace crossed his face. "I'll have to do all my laughing in my thoughts for a while," he said as his expression smoothed.

"Welcome back to the land of the living." Graham grinned.

"I was pretty sure I'd had it this time."

"We weren't so sure about you for a while either," the detective answered.

"What happened after I was shot? All I recall is a jumble of voices."

Ryder's gaze pierced Carina. Her stomach clenched. Did he remember her impulsive declaration of love? She squirmed on the inside. She'd meant the words with her whole heart and hadn't changed her mind, but it wasn't realistic to expect him to reciprocate so soon in their acquaintance. Especially when she was mind-boggled at herself for falling so fast and hard for him. Nearly losing him had forced her to recognize the true state of her heart. But she still needed to be certain her feelings weren't rooted in her admiration and gratitude for his bravery and self-sacrifice on her behalf. She didn't think so, but only time would tell.

Patience. The word was both a balm and an irritant when she craved a little space to develop confidence in her feelings and yet desperately needed to know if he felt the same way. Was there a future for them?

"A jumble of voices." Graham snorted a laugh. "A pretty fair description of that big circus. As soon as I got your voicemail that you were going to Carina's aunt's place, and you were suspicious of the situation, my partner and I headed out after you and brought a couple of uniforms along. Call it a gut reaction to your gut feeling."

"Very good thing you did," Carina said with a smile at Graham. Then she turned toward Ryder. "They burst into the house right after you got shot, called for ambulances, delivered first aid to the wounded and stopped my cousin Frank from escaping all in one orchestrated flurry."

"What about the contract killer?" Ryder asked.

The detective smirked. "Your bullet grazed his temple. Knocked him cold. We scooped him right up, but the FBI swooped in and carted him off as soon as the hospital was ready to discharge him. He's got law enforcement in nine different countries waiting their turn at him."

"The bad guys are getting what they deserve and then some." Carina put her hand over Ryder's and he closed his fingers around hers. Her heart warmed. Her cheeks, too, but she schooled her expression to pretend not to notice. "In expectation of a lighter sentence, my cousin tops the list of those spilling all he knows about his father."

"Ouch! That's got to bite old Orlando Spinx." Ryder's grin said he appreciated the poetic justice. "Abandon your kid, and then when it counts the most, the kid abandons you." He licked his lips. "Any water around here?"

Carina quickly put the straw to Ryder's mouth and he sucked a few gulps.

"Thank you," he said. "Now, would you answer a burning question for me?"

She resisted squirming under the kind of scrutiny she could only describe as a cop stare. "What?"

"Did you trip over that chair on purpose?"

"It was a lame move, I know." A tiny laugh spurted between her lips. "But I wasn't about to be led quietly into a vehicle with our friendly neighborhood hit man."

"Not lame at all." Ryder beamed at her. "Your fancy footwork likely saved our lives."

"Brilliant," said Detective Graham.

Carina's face heated, but she met Ryder's steady stare. "Only because you took over from there."

"The lady is modest." Graham chuckled.

A knock drew their attention to the door. Ryder's doctor stepped inside and fixed the bed with a look rendered owlish by thick-lensed, oversize glasses. "Excellent, I see my patient is awake. If you visitors would wait outside for a little while, I need to examine him."

Graham waved at Ryder. "I need to return to work for now anyway, but I'll be back later to get your official statement."

"One more thing before you go." Ryder lifted a hand. "Did Hicks ever give up what he was hiding during the initial interview? Something more about Carina's kidnapping?"

"You knew he was hiding something?"

"I had a feeling."

Graham snorted. "I'm coming to respect your feelings big-time. Yeah, both Hicks and Trainer embellished their stories as soon as they found out who we had in custody. You're not hardly going to believe this." The detective's eyes slid toward Carina and then darted away. "Spinx was a part of that whole affair with Carina's family."

Oxygen vacated her lungs and she pressed the heel of her hand to her chest. "Spinx?"

"You got it." The detective nodded. "He was barely more than a thug himself twenty years ago, but up and coming in the criminal organization. The diamond heist was his brainstorm, but Trainer muffed it." Graham met Carina's riveted stare. "Spinx was present at least part of the time his buddies were interrogating you—and wearing a gorilla mask."

Carina's eyes fell away to rest on Ryder.

His eyes were soft upon her. "What a tangled web of connections, with one big spider at the center."

Carina shook her head. "Despite the spider, God orchestrated this resolution, bringing goodness and justice out of tragedy and hurt." She squeezed his hand and let it go. "Visit with your doctor now. I'll be back in the morning. I need to spend time with my son."

Ryder smiled. "Jace is all right?"

"Jace is terrific."

"Bring him with you when you come back."

"If you think you can handle an active toddler in the room." She glanced at the doctor, who shrugged and then nodded.

Ryder offered her that lopsided grin that always gave her pulse a kick start. "I can handle peekaboo. Tag will have to wait awhile."

Carina left the room with her heart soaring like a helium balloon released from its string. His words implied he anticipated an ongoing association between them.

Please, God, let it be so.

* * *

As the doctor quietly left the room after pronouncing him on the mend, Ryder settled back against his pillow. Supper was promised soon, and his stomach was more than ready for food, but his eyelids were heavy. Maybe he'd grab a nap while he waited for the meal. His eyes closed, and a smile settled on his lips. Carina was coming back. She wasn't ready to cut him loose now that she was safe.

Did that mean she'd be open to a relationship of the romantic variety with him? Surely he couldn't have heard what he thought he'd heard her say when he'd been about to pass out at her aunt's house. But what if he *had* heard right? No, the dream was too good to be true. He'd better give it some time and sound her out a bit before he made his own confession of feelings. He was pretty sure he'd only thought the words but had not said them aloud before darkness claimed him on that kitchen floor. The last thing he wanted to do was scare her away.

Slipping into slumber began to quiet his mind, but then his bedside telephone let out a jangle. On the third ring, Ryder managed to put the headset to his ear and state a groggy hello. The voice on the other end brought him to attention quickly. Stan Jeffers, Chief of

Police from the Oklahoma City Police Department. By cop standards, it was roughly like getting a telephone call from the governor of their state.

"Congratulations on bringing down that cockroach Spinx," the man boomed in his ear, not bothering with small talk. "We're all breathing easier in OKC. A guy like you can't stop being a cop even when he's not on the payroll." He let out a husky chuckle. "When are you ready to officially get back on the job?"

Ryder's mouth went drier than it had been the first time he'd hazily roused after surgery. *Was* he going back? His heart knew the answer. He was a cop. Always had been a cop. Always would be a cop. He'd been fooling himself to think he could walk away and do something else.

"Soon, I think," he said. "I'll let you know."

"Do that," Jeffers answered. "Heal fast. We've got lots to pile on your plate when you get here."

The man chuckled again and then a click let Ryder know the busy chief had ended the call abruptly.

Mind racing, Ryder stared at the handset. Then his supper arrived and he gave the meal his undivided attention.

After dinner, a pair of nurses came in and saw to it that he got up and took a little walk. When Ryder returned to his room, hollowed out by an aggravating level of fatigue but fed up with bedrest, he eased into the armchair by the window and watched dusk settle over the city of Tulsa. If he went back to Oklahoma City and Carina went back to Argyle, what would that mean for exploring any relationship they might have?

Sure, he'd visit frequently in Argyle to see his mother in the care center and take Carina out, but would that level of contact be enough to nurture what they were starting to develop together? And what if his mom consented to move into a care center closer to where her daughter—his sister—lived? That idea had been in the discussion stage for a while. Would the necessity of dividing his off-hour traveling time between going to see his mother and visiting Carina be a problem? Almost certainly. His stomach knotted.

A knock brought his head around. Detective Graham strode in, sporting pouches of weariness under reddened eyes like badges of honor above a triumphant grin. Ryder well knew the successful-closure-of-a-case syndrome.

"Things are wrapping up nicely, I take it," Ryder said.

"Beyond imagination. Not only do we put a ribbon on a twenty-year-old double homicide and child kidnapping case *and* catch a notorious contract killer, but between the feds and police departments scattered across multiple states, we're in the process of dismantling the biggest criminal organization infecting America's breadbasket. Lots of good folks are going to be sleeping better tonight. I'm on my way home to grab some shut-eye myself."

"You're not here for my statement?"

"Tomorrow." Graham waved the idea away. "The chief wanted me to come by tonight to make sure we get our job offer to you first. How would you like to join the Tulsa PD? You'd receive a warm welcome."

A chuckle attempted to bloom in Ryder's chest, but a jab of pain tamped it down. "You're too late to be first. The OKC chief called me right before supper all but ordering me to get back to work for him."

Graham's face fell.

Ryder lifted a hand. "Take it easy. I haven't decided anything yet. I'm honored by the offer from the Tulsa PD."

"So you'll consider it?" The detective brightened.

"I will."

With a wave, Graham strode away. If Ryder

wasn't mistaken, the guy was humming under his breath.

Ryder shook his head, grinning. Then he sobered as implications unfolded in his mind. Maybe if he lived in Tulsa, Carina would consider coming back here—but not moving in with her aunt. There must be tons of accounting jobs in this city. The same applied to OKC, but either way, it wasn't fair of him to expect her to move anywhere else but where she'd already landed a job. So where did that leave Carina and him?

The questions and nuances of possibilities kept Ryder's sleep fitful overnight, but he woke up ready to be done with bedrest. After a welcome but cautiously executed shower and shave, he managed to put on a pair of jeans and a loose-fitting T-shirt Carina had thoughtfully left for him yesterday. The doctor came in and satisfied himself that Ryder's wound remained clear of infection.

"If you maintain this rate of healing, I'd be willing to let you go in a day or two," the man said and then bustled on toward the next patient.

The doctor had no sooner left than the pitter-patter of tiny feet and unintelligible jabber of toddler talk alerted him that Carina and Jace were approaching his room. Ryder settled in the seat by the window and had his smile ready when Jace chugged into the room.

"I'der!" the boy cried out and trotted toward him, chubby arms outstretched.

Ryder's heart turned inside out. This kid was the poster child for cute.

His mother caught his hand. "Slowly, young man. Remember, I told you Ryder has an ouchy."

Jace slowed, came to a stop and leaned against Ryder's knees, gazing up at him with big eyes.

"Ryder will be better soon," he told the little boy. He covered his face with his hands then suddenly spread them apart.

A toothy giggle answered him. "'Eek!"

"Peek. That's right," his mother said and picked him up mid attempt to scramble onto Ryder's lap.

"You have no idea how much I wish I could laugh." He shook his head.

"All in good time, young man," Carina answered with a mock prim look.

Movement behind her caught Ryder's attention. "Hello, Althea." The older woman was lurking just inside the doorway. "Come on in."

Althea moved closer but kept her eyes averted. "I came to apologize."

"For what?" he asked.

"My son. My ex-husband." The woman lifted her head, exposing red-rimmed eyes. "This should never have happened, and my behavior caused it."

Ryder shook his head. "Those with evil bent will always find an excuse to act out their nature."

Carina gave a small laugh. "Is that some sort of proverb?"

"Maybe a cop proverb." Ryder stopped himself barely in time from attempting a shrug.

Carina turned to her aunt. "I understand your desire to protect your loved ones. Some things that happened to you caused the natural instinct to get out of control. No one blames you."

Althea's shoulders squared. "It may take a while before I believe that and can accept God's forgiveness. But you should know my motives weren't so totally selfless as protecting those I love. Most of all, I was trying to protect myself from the loneliness that comes from not being needed. I was trying to force people to need me." She inhaled a deep breath and gusted it out. "I've called a Christian counseling agency and have an appointment for tomorrow. I want you to know, Carina, that I'm going to work hard to respect your boundaries from now on."

Tears stung the backs of Ryder's eyes. Carina's cheeks were wet with them.

She stepped forward and wrapped her aunt in a hug. "You *are* needed and loved."

Sniffling and wiping at her face with the palms of her hands, Althea stepped back. "If it's okay with you, I'll take Jace and let you and Ryder talk."

Carina nodded, and the older woman lifted the toddler into her arms. The pair headed out of the room, Jace waving and grinning over his great-aunty's shoulder.

Carina pulled up a chair, perched in front of Ryder and regarded him soberly. "I need to head back to Argyle today. When we knew you came out of surgery okay, I finally remembered to call my boss at the farmers' co-op and let him know what was going on. He was appalled and sympathetic and had no problem putting off my start date by a few days, but I promised him I'd be in the office tomorrow."

"Where will you live?"

"A hotel until I can find another place. I already had day care lined up for Jace, so that's where he'll be while I'm at work. You don't have to worry about us. We'll be fine."

Ryder's heart sank. She was pushing him away.

She shifted in her seat and dropped her gaze.

"What's next for you? I mean… I'm getting the vibe from the folks at the Tulsa PD that they'd like you to come work for them."

"Yes, I've had a job offer. Had a call from OKC, too. They want me back."

"Which job are you going to take?"

"I don't know. Maybe neither."

"Really?"

Was he mistaken or had her face briefly lit up? She'd gone perfectly sober again, but did that fleeting expression mean she hoped he wouldn't move to Tulsa or Oklahoma City? Or maybe it meant she didn't think he should go back to being a cop.

"Should I not join the force again?"

She blinked at him. "You need to do what you're wired to do. The world will be a poorer place if you don't."

"Thanks. I'm glad you're good with it."

"Why would *I* need to be good with it?"

Their gazes met and held. Hers shimmered with a muted brightness, like cautious expectation mingled with half-frightened hope. He could be wrong—he didn't want to be wrong—but that was what he read in her face. Was she inviting him to take a risk?

Ryder sucked in a breath. "Did you mean it?"

Understanding blanketed her expression.

She knew exactly what he was asking. With a visible gulp, she slowly nodded.

Oxygen gushed from Ryder's lungs and he slumped against the chair. A sharp pain in his chest met the movement, but he couldn't care less. His heart soared on eagle's wings.

"I said it, too," he told her. "But only in my head. I couldn't get the words out."

"Say it to me now." Her amber gaze captured him.

"I love you, Carina Collins."

Her smile was incandescent. She sprang from her chair and bent over him. Ryder leaned forward and met her halfway in a warm and tender meeting of lips and hearts. He knew exactly which job he was going to take—the one that kept him close to her.

EPILOGUE

Nine months later

Smiling, Carina waved goodbye to the sweet and wonderful woman beaming back at her from the care center bed and joined Ryder walking up the tastefully decorated hall away from his mother's room. From a perch in Ryder's arms, Jace was jabbering a mile a minute about wanting to see the "birdies" in the aviary maintained by the care center in its inviting sunroom. They'd already been there once today, with Ryder's mother in her wheelchair, but Jace could never get enough of the flitting, chirping birds.

"Shall we?" Ryder cocked a brow at her.

"How can we say no to such an innocent request?"

"Birdies it is," he told Jace, who squealed and wiggled to be let down.

"Hold on there, buddy," Ryder told him. "I'll turn you loose when we get there."

Carina gazed at the grinning pair. Surely, the love that filled her heart for them was beyond anything she could possibly deserve, but thankfully, where God's blessings were concerned, deserving wasn't part of the equation. The old nightmares had ceased, and even the tiny bare spot in her memories no longer bothered her. She had the answers she'd needed to fill in the blanks—thanks in large part to this man beside her. And for him, flashbacks to the OKC bombing were now a rarity.

Ryder had bounced back quickly to health and vigor from his near-fatal gunshot wound, and had been a detective with the Argyle police department for the past eight months. When Ryder came on board, Detective Worthing crowed like he'd put one over on the big-city departments, but Carina had been a little nervous about the change of pace for Ryder. She needn't have worried. He seemed genuinely happy with his choice of career in small-town America. However, as the loved one of a member of law enforcement, Carina had been a bit dismayed to discover the amount of crime police dealt with outside the metro areas. Who knew? Ryder's motto was "the crooks don't rest, nor do the cops who catch them."

He'd been busier than she'd thought possible, but at least his home renovation project was done, and his mother's house was on the market. Carina had long ago found another rental home to live in, and she was enjoying her job with the farmers' cooperative. She'd made many friends at her workplace and at the small church she and Ryder attended. What more could she want?

Well, maybe one thing: house hunting with Ryder. They both favored a ranch-style. But a wedding needed to happen before they could make a purchase and move in together. Was she too impatient while he was being too cautious? He was always more than careful not to pressure her about their relationship, and she appreciated that, but she was about ready to tell him, "Get on with it, already."

Maybe she should go ahead and propose to *him*. A giggle escaped her lips. Wouldn't Aunt Althea have a fit? Not because the woman would object to the match. She adored Ryder. And she was valiantly avoiding any hint of attempting to control Carina's life any longer. No, the reaction would simply be from her traditional ways.

They arrived in the sunroom and Ryder released the squirming twenty-seven-month-old bundle as promised. Jace scurried to the aviary and watched with rapt eyes as the bright-colored birds flew from branch to branch and nest to nest, trilling at one another.

Ryder's warm fingers closed around Carina's, and she looked up at him. That half grin of his inspired the usual *ka-bump* of her heart.

"You seem particularly happy today," he said as he drew her toward a cozy seating alcove.

"Why do you say that?" She snuggled up beside him on a small love seat.

He planted a soft kiss on her lips then pulled back. "You were laughing to yourself a minute ago."

"I was enjoying an absurd thought."

"Do tell."

Should she tell? Why not? They were always honest with each other. The worst he could do was laugh and pass the moment off lightly. She'd be okay with that because she didn't want to pressure him either.

"I was thinking about *me* proposing to *you*." She picked an imaginary bit of lint from her slacks.

"Oh, really?" Ryder lifted her chin with cupped fingers. Their gazes met. He was smiling but not laughing. "I was going to wait until tonight when we were out for dinner together, but now I see that scenario is entirely too cliché for the likes of us."

Carina's breathing went shallow as his hand dove into the pocket of his lightweight jacket.

"How about here and now?" He opened the small box he held out to her. A ruby set within a circle of emeralds shimmered back at her. No diamonds. Never those. "Carina Collins, will you complete my life by marrying me?"

Carina held her hand out to him, welcoming the ring. "The sooner, the better, my love."

"Oooh, pwetty!" Jace's little voice came from close in front of them as Ryder slipped the band around her finger.

"Hello, buddy." Ryder put his hand on Jace's shoulder. "Is it all right with you if I marry your mommy?" He turned to Carina. "Does he know what that means?"

She nodded. "I've explained the idea to him on several occasions in as many ways as I know how."

"Wight." Jace bobbed his head at Ryder, a sage expression on his face. "Means I can cow you Daddy."

"That's absolutely the truth, buddy." Tears shimmering in his eyes, Ryder scooped the little boy onto his lap.

Carina's eyes filled with moisture as his strong arms wrapped them in a three-way hug.

She'd wait until their date tonight to collect Ryder's tender kisses. For now, she inhaled deeply of Jace's little-boy sweat and her fiancé's outdoorsy shampoo.

Best. Family. Ever.

* * * * *

If you enjoyed this story, look for these other books by Jill Elizabeth Nelson:

In Need of Protection
Hunted for Christmas

Dear Reader,

Thank you for stepping into Carina and Ryder's world and joining them for a wild ride full of heartache and healing. Both Carina and Ryder are challenged to make sense of the tragedies that have happened to them—much like we are when our lives careen off course through events beyond our control. The pair eventually find hope and significance, forgiveness and release in trusting God with the unanswerable questions and in giving their love to each other. A new family is formed in the crucible of suffering weathered with courage and faith.

My prayer for you is that you will find the same courage in the midst of suffering and the comfort only faith in God can provide. May His peace fill you regardless of your circumstances past, present or future. And may you be released from bitterness by the key of forgiveness for self and others, and in trusting God's sure justice.

I enjoy hearing from my readers. My email address is jnelson@jillelizabethnelson.com. I can also be contacted through my Facebook

page at Facebook.com/JillElizabethNelson.
Author. Looking forward to hearing from you!

Abundant blessings,
Jill

Get 4 FREE REWARDS!

We'll send you 2 FREE Books plus 2 FREE Mystery Gifts.

FREE Value Over **$20**

Both the **Harlequin® Special Edition** and **Harlequin® Heartwarming™** series feature compelling novels filled with stories of love and strength where the bonds of friendship, family and community unite.

YES! Please send me 2 FREE novels from the Harlequin Special Edition or Harlequin Heartwarming series and my 2 FREE gifts (gifts are worth about $10 retail). After receiving them, if I don't wish to receive any more books, I can return the shipping statement marked "cancel." If I don't cancel, I will receive 6 brand-new Harlequin Special Edition books every month and be billed just $4.99 each in the U.S or $5.74 each in Canada, a savings of at least 17% off the cover price or 4 brand-new Harlequin Heartwarming Larger-Print books every month and be billed just $5.74 each in the U.S. or $6.24 each in Canada, a savings of at least 21% off the cover price. It's quite a bargain! Shipping and handling is just 50¢ per book in the U.S. and $1.25 per book in Canada.* I understand that accepting the 2 free books and gifts places me under no obligation to buy anything. I can always return a shipment and cancel at any time. The free books and gifts are mine to keep no matter what I decide.

Choose one: ☐ **Harlequin Special Edition**
(235/335 HDN GNMP)

☐ **Harlequin Heartwarming**
Larger-Print
(161/361 HDN GNPZ)

Name (please print)

Address _____ Apt. #

City _____ State/Province _____ Zip/Postal Code

Email: Please check this box ☐ if you would like to receive newsletters and promotional emails from Harlequin Enterprises ULC and its affiliates. You can unsubscribe anytime.

Mail to the **Harlequin Reader Service:**

IN U.S.A.: P.O. Box 1341, Buffalo, NY 14240-8531
IN CANADA: P.O. Box 603, Fort Erie, Ontario L2A 5X3

Want to try 2 free books from another series! Call 1-800-873-8635 or visit www.ReaderService.com.

Visit ReaderService.com Today!

As a valued member of the Harlequin Reader Service, you'll find these benefits and more at ReaderService.com:

- Try 2 free books from any series
- Access risk-free special offers
- View your account history & manage payments
- Browse the latest Bonus Bucks catalog

Don't miss out!

If you want to stay up-to-date on the latest at the Harlequin Reader Service and enjoy more content, make sure you've signed up for our monthly News & Notes email newsletter. Sign up online at ReaderService.com or by calling Customer Service at 1-800-873-8635.

RS20